WINTER ROAD

A NOVELLA

KRISTINA RIENZI

WINTER ROAD

Copyright © 2015 Kristina Rienzi

All rights reserved. No part of this book may be reproduced, transmitted, stored, scanned or distributed in any printed or electronic form, whole or in part by any means, without express written permission from the publisher. Please purchase only authorized editions and do not participate in piracy of copyrighted materials in violation of author's rights.

Book Layout: Kate Tilton (www.katetilton.com)

Cover Design: Kari March Designs (www.KariMarch.com)

Author Photograph: Jaime Lynn Photography (www.JaimeLynnPhotography.com)

Publisher's Note: This is a work of fiction. Names, characters, places, and incidents are a product of the author's creative imagination. Locales and public names are sometimes used for atmospheric purposes. Any resemblance to actual people, living or dead, or to businesses, companies, events, institutions, or locales is completely coincidental.

INDIGO HAWK GROUP

PRINTED IN THE UNITED STATES OF AMERICA

ISBN: 978-0-9969721-5-4

This book is dedicated to my parents who taught me how to live with the spirit of Christmas in my heart all year long.

And all I loved, I loved alone.
—EDGAR ALLAN POE

MORE SO THAN the chill in the air, the frozen pieces of my heart summoned me back to Winter Road. My family's snow-covered and deer-trodden property in the back woods of Shady Knolls, New Jersey, was the only place I wanted to be, surrounded by my most treasured memories and people.

When the weather turned brisk for good, and there was no chance of a break in the frigid temperatures, I longed to be miles away from the hustlers of my bustling metropolis. The buzz of the city drained me entirely. By any given December, it was all too much to handle, and this year more so than ever.

As I maneuvered my truck, making the long trek up the dirt and gravel driveway I used to call my home, my anxiety waned. It was as if there was an invisible harness pulling me closer to the ones I loved most. Instantly, all of my problems seemed to melt away.

My childhood home was North Pole worthy, with multi-colored, giant LED lights strung around each window, lining the roof and framing the double doors to its entrance. I didn't even have to step foot in the backyard to know exactly what it looked like—a spitting image of every year that had come before it: a winter wonderland, complete with a giant fire pit and marshmallows at the ready.

A pang of guilt grasped my heart. I've been away much too long. I haven't come home nearly enough.

Life had been more than challenging for the Montgomery family of late with Mom's increasing health issues, Dad's recent financial troubles, along with Matt and Kate's endless fertility struggles. It was no wonder my family considered me their golden child. I couldn't blame them. As far as they knew, I was a superstar in the Manhattan commercial real-estate business. Not to mention, I was engaged to one of the most insanely handsome and wealthy bachelors in the city. Jake was the man every girl dreamed about marrying, and I had landed him.

Like they say, be careful what you wish for because life isn't always what it seems.

My SUV's navigation screen flashed to telephone mode. The number made me shudder. I promptly hit the end button on my steering wheel. I have seventeen voicemails already, what's one more?

I didn't have to listen to the messages because I was pretty sure they were all some form of, "Amelia, call me back. I demand it."

Suit yourself. Demand away.

My parents' old house, with its rainbow lights winking at me, welcomed me home. As I drew nearer, my insides warmed. In my mind's eye, I was already curled up in front of the stone fireplace with an old, furry blanket across my lap. I had a giant slab of cinnamon apple pie in one hand, and a steaming mug of herbal tea, spiked, of course, in the other. Most importantly, I was surrounded by the safety and comfort of my family all around me.

I shifted the truck into park and shut off the engine. As if on cue, the front door flew open. Dad came out on the porch, waving as though I hadn't seen him standing there.

He yelled to me, "Hey, buttercup, you made it." Even from the driveway, I could see how his smile was wrapped in wrinkles, age getting the better of him.

"Sure did." I plodded through the snow to him for a long-overdue giant hug. We held on a few seconds longer than usual. Our embrace affirmed my suspicion. It had been much too long since my last visit. They needed me here.

"Matt, Mel's here. Help us out, would you?" My dad didn't wait for my brother. He started grabbing my bags out of the car.

Kate greeted me first. "Hey, lady." She kissed me on the cheek and I returned the sentiment. I loved my sister-in-law, which was a blessing and more than most could say of their in-laws.

"How are you?" It wasn't a generic question. Kate had been through hell and had come back with third-degree burns.

"I'm good. Really good." Her genuine smile reached her eyes. "It's wonderful to see you."

Matt, my giant football-star-turned-small-town-banker brother, came around behind Kate and bear-hugged me away from her.

"Jeez, Matt. Don't crush her," Kate said before heading back into the living room.

"For Christ's sake, Mel. You're skin and bones. Get in the kitchen and eat something, you hear me?" Matt hit me on the shoulder before heading off to help Dad.

"It's called being healthy." I immediately regretted my

words when I turned and saw my mom. Thirty pounds lighter than my last visit, she stood waif-like in the kitchen. Tears welled up in my eyes without warning. I blinked them back, smiling. "Hey, Ma." I hugged her, not too tight and not too long, even though I never wanted to let her go.

She wasn't okay. We both knew it.

"How's my girl?" She hugged me again, only this time she was the one to squeeze harder. I gave in.

She had been battling heart disease for years, but this was something else. I wasn't sure why she hadn't told me, maybe she didn't know herself exactly what was wrong, but my heart sensed it wasn't anything good.

Instead of broaching a terrible diagnosis I didn't want to consider, I asked, "How are you feeling?"

She shrugged. "I'm good, Sweetie. Don't you worry about me, okay?"

"Me? Worry about you? Never. You're the strongest one out of all of us." I was lying, of course. I worried all the damn time. She was my mother, after all. Worry was an understatement.

"Where's that handsome fiancé of yours? Getting bags out of the car with the boys?" Mom always called the men in our family the boys. I supposed it was her way of keeping us young in her eyes.

I bit my lip. "Jake couldn't come tonight."

"Aw, I'm sorry to hear it, Honey. Well, you make sure to send him our love when you talk to him. And don't forget to take his gifts home with you." Mom pointed a few times to a pile of presents under the tree. She always went overboard when it came to the holidays, even on our birthdays, but mostly for Christmas. She had a way of making everyone she met feel like they were the most special person in the universe.

"Of course," I said, as I poured myself a hefty glass of my favorite spin on eggnog: coquito.

I hated lying to her, but she didn't need to know the truth tonight. The last thing I wanted was for my family to worry about me on Christmas, especially my mom who had enough worries for one person to last a lifetime.

After the holidays, when things settled down, I'd tell everyone the truth. Jake Grayson didn't end up being at all what he seemed, or had promised. Sure, he was striking, wealthy beyond measure and, as far as he had said, madly in love with me. I shouldn't have complained, and I wasn't any longer.

It was finally over between us.

As it turned out, perfection of Jake's kind came with a hefty price tag—one I was never going to be willing to pay.

This year, I hadn't simply come home for the holidays. I was running away from the worst decision I had ever made.

CHAPTER TWO

THE HIGH END three-piece suit hung beautifully in Jake's closet, with its exquisite navy hue and barely there pinstripes. It was simply the perfect outfit for the holiday.

Jake sighed. The poor thing was pressed and begging to be worn, especially with its companion crisp white shirt and crimson tie. With lips pursed, he looked over his preferred ensemble one last time, pained that he wouldn't be wearing it tonight. If he did, he would be overdressed to a fault.

Priding himself on being a cut above his fellow guests when it came to couture, he needed to look flawless, play the part and, most importantly, fit in. This evening was far too important for him to risk screwing up.

Besides, it was Christmas Eve. He wasn't about to take any chances---not with anything.

Jake rolled his eyes as he pushed the costly suit aside. Of course, he would rather have spent the holiday at one of the five-star hotels by Central Park, dining amongst the city's most elite, but it wasn't going to happen this year. Once they were married, Amelia wouldn't have any choice in the matter.

In compromise, Jake opted for his highest-end wool blazer. If he coupled it with the right cashmere sweater vest and button-down shirt combination, added a pair of dark designer jeans and overpriced cowboy boots, he would feel like himself without completely overdoing it. His outfit would still cost more than all of the Montgomery family's clothing combined, but no one would be the wiser. He would look average, like Amelia's family.

Jake checked his phone again. He needed to make sure his cell was charged and the ringer was on its loudest setting. Sadly, both were the case and, still, he hadn't missed any calls. There were no text messages either. All the same, he would be speaking with his love in person soon enough.

After Jake was fully dressed, and he was absolutely certain not a hair was out of place on his gorgeous head, he stepped in front of the full-length mirror to get a good eyeful of himself. Even he was impressed at how well he had pulled off the average-normal-guy look. He was far from average looking, and far from normal; two truths he loved about himself. But, he had done it, and it was all for his soon-to-be-wife, Amelia.

Jake glanced at his watch. He had a little over two hours until Christmas Eve dinner was served at the Montgomery's table. Typically, it took about an hour to get there without traffic. But, of course, on a holiday there would be plenty of cars clogging up the roadways. In his estimation, he had approximately five minutes to get on the road if he wanted to arrive at Amelia's parent's house on time.

Speeding wasn't an option tonight. While he had always found a way to talk himself out of a ticket, he had no stomach for dealing with the hassle of it all, especially since he would be under the influence of alcohol. *Slower was better*. That way, he could plan out the night in his mind, prepare for all possible scenarios, and ensure nothing was left to chance.

Jake smiled at his sinister thoughts. *It's all about control.*

The last decision Jake had to make, and arguably the most important, was choosing two things: the ideal whiskey to offer for the Montgomery's festivities, and the exemplary one to drink on the long ride into the mountains of New Jersey.

Fingering his assortment of bottles, he paused on a mid-priced Irish whiskey, which he chose for the family. It would more than do, as it was one of the best for their caliber of taste.

Then he settled on one of his favorites for the drive—a rare, peaty scotch whiskey to relax him, while sharpening his mind at the same time. Jake was a strategic and creative thinker when he drank, and his internal editor, who told him not to do things, was dead asleep.

In truth, Jake wasn't worried at all about the upcoming evening. In fact, he had already predicted with certainty exactly how it would turn out. Jake was a decision maker by nature—driven and resolute. When he made his mind up about something, there was absolutely no turning back. In more ways than one, Jake had made up his mind about tonight. And no matter the course he took, the night was destined to end in his favor.

Jake grabbed his duffle bag, threw on his coat, and set the alarm on his penthouse.

After handing the doorman a cool hundred-dollar bill, Jake took the short walk around the block to where he had parked his newly purchased, in cash of course, used sedan. It was unassuming, exactly the way he needed it to be. He popped the trunk and threw in his leather duffle, which was filled with the perfect items for his Plan A: gifts, whiskey and overnight attire.

But before closing the lid, he paused to admire the other contents, the ones required for his Plan B. He smiled at the rope, handcuffs, drill, syringes, duct tape and, of course, the oversized locked box stocked with various firearms. He wasn't sure which weapons would be required and which ones would prove useless. Jake figured he was better off bringing all of them. It wasn't as though he had practice in committing mass civilian homicide. But, if the night called for it, then he would gladly add it to his already stellar military resume.

Plan for the worst while forcing the best was Jake's motto.

Sometimes the finest original plans weren't meant to be, and equally optimal alternatives must be explored. Taking on a family of five wasn't his first choice for the holiday, but he would do whatever needed to be done when it came to possessing Amelia.

If Amelia wasn't going to be with Jake willingly, he would have no choice but to force the situation until being with him was the only option she had.

If that didn't work, then, sadly, Amelia would belong to no one.

CHAPTER THREE

LONG BEFORE RUSTIC decor was in style, my mom had it down to a science, even more so at the holidays than any other time of year. The red cinnamon-scented candles, old-fashioned oil lamps, pinecones, and perfect greenery adorned her simple wooden table, which was fancied up in its cream holiday linens and purposely mismatched stoneware. Every dinner guest had a unique setting, a creative spin my mom put on her use of old garage sale finds. She was nothing if not thrifty, resourceful, and thoughtful.

My dad and Matt were on the couch, drinks in hand, while Kate joined my mom and me in the dining room. We were adding the final touches, lighting candles and such, before we announced it was time for dinner.

"How can I help?" Kate asked.

"Honey, you've done enough, but thank you for asking. Go ahead and relax a bit." My mom made a gesture for Kate to sit down.

"Can I get you a drink?" I grabbed the red wine, my sister-in-law's favorite, but she shook her head.

I let it go, knowing Kate was most likely going through one of her fertility treatment cycles. I didn't want to make her feel the need to explain herself, yet again. My parents had long ago resolved themselves to me not reproducing, being a *professional person* and all, which meant making babies was all up to Matt and Kate, and that was a lot of pressure for a couple.

I switched to wine, pouring myself a glass instead. Being double fisted at the holidays was a given. I put my coquito aside, and drank down a quarter of the Pinot Noir in one gulp. A hell of a week was behind me, and I was still wavering with how honest I needed to be when it came to my lack of a relationship with Jake. I reminded myself it was the holidays and I'd be forgiven in the New Year if I lied for the greater festive good. Besides, I didn't want to make tonight about me because it was about all of us: The Montgomery family.

When steam was rising above our dinner and everyone was in their respective seats, we said a little prayer, blessing our food and our souls. Most of us weren't religious, but Mom was, and we always indulged her rituals because when she was happy, it made us happy, too.

As soon as we picked up our forks, Matt stood up and asked for our attention. We all turned our heads, obliging. With one hand on Kate and the other on his wine, he raised his glass in the air. "Appropriate or not, something needs to be said." He whispered to his wife, "Please forgive me." He pulled her up to standing, too.

"What are you doing?" Kate's face grew pink.

"Honey, you've been through so much over the years. I want this holiday to be incredibly special for all of us."

Kate's eyes grew wide and she opened her mouth as if to speak, but exhaled instead, giving in to her husband.

I glanced over at my mom and dad who had scrunched faces as if they were both confused and concerned. I prayed the news Matt was about to share was going to be good. I'd already decided to spare everyone the agony of my life and hoped Matt would do the same. God Forbid either of them was sick, or they had decided to get a divorce. I honestly didn't think our parents could handle such news, especially not at our Christmas Eve dinner.

I held my breath for what was to come.

Matt turned to us and said, "Kate's pregnant."

A pause, and then a giant sigh of relief fell over the room. My mom got up and walked around to their side of the table, hugging and kissing them both. Dad followed suit.

I stood up and made my way over to them, unsure of what to say. I was ecstatic, of course. It was what we all wanted—a baby to bring us joy and love and hope. But, Kate hadn't been lucky in the past and it had brought them a tremendous amount of pain. They had been through hell. More than hell, they had been tortured repeatedly with loss. It was clear neither of them planned to reveal the news, understandably afraid something might go wrong with the pregnancy as it had in the past.

Matt's face told us the story—they needed to *try* to be happy. They had to believe it was possible for them to have a family. And he was going to celebrate the good news no matter the outcome.

In truth, we all needed to be happy—even if only for the holidays.

I gave Kate a colossal hug and told her how incredibly happy I was for the both of them. She smiled back, the faint tears in her eyes twinkling in gratitude and fear.

After everyone got in their hugs and kisses, we all took our respective seats at the table and dove into deliciousness.

About fifteen minutes into the meal, there was a knock at the door.

"Who else is coming?" I asked, a little panicked.

Matt got up. "No one we invited. I'll take care of it."

It's not like someone could happen upon my parent's house. It was set at the end of a long driveway, several hundred feet away from Winter Road. The only people who ever came to the door were invited guests or delivery persons.

Matt opened the door, and I turned around to find out who had decided to crash our holiday. I gasped, nearly falling off my chair. It was a face I had no intention of running into ever again. One I had tried to forget all about. One I assumed had forgotten all about me.

I quickly spun my head around and went back to my dinner, pretending I hadn't noticed.

"Come on in, Billy." My mom stood and went to the cabinet to grab a plate.

I tried to whisper and smile, but I spoke through gritted teeth. "What are you doing?"

"Shh." She shooed me off before turning her attention toward the front door. "Have a seat. You can't come over on Christmas Eve and not have a meal with us. Sit down and eat, won't you?"

Billy never stood a chance when it came to my mother. We dated for two years in high school, a long time in our short lives, and our families were close. She loved him like he was her own son. I had always known it, and it was one of the many reasons breaking up with him broke my heart. It seemed unnatural to separate him from our lives at the time, but I was convinced I had outgrown Shady Knolls and it was time for me to move on. Now, I wasn't so sure.

Billy took the seat directly across from me. I half smiled. "Hey."

"Hey." He wore the same slanted smile that jumpstarted my heart back in time ten years.

"Glad you stopped by," Dad said. "It's snowing pretty good out there."

I hadn't noticed. I lifted up off my chair a bit to peer out the kitchen window. Sure enough, it was coming down even harder than when I had arrived.

"I figured you weren't plowing anything tonight, so I stopped by to take care of it for you."

Dad patted him on the back. "You're a good man, Billy. You'll always have a seat at our table."

Billy had never left Shady Knolls when the rest of us went off to start our lives in one town or another. Instead, he had opted for the admirable road and took over his family's business after his father passed away our senior year of high school. My mom had always kept in touch with the Campbells, and I remembered her saying Billy had moved back into his parents' house a few years ago when his mother also passed away. My parents felt so badly at the time that they hired him, vowing to always give him business and a place he could call home, an extended family of sorts. It should have bothered me, with him being my ex-boyfriend, but it didn't. It felt good. Billy was a good guy. We had a good relationship. It didn't end badly, it just ended—a natural progression for me into another phase in life. Maybe I was being selfish at the time, but I was only eighteen and it had made sense for me to go off to college and then work in the city. I didn't want a guy back home holding me back.

Billy had taken it harder. He was willing to do anything to be together. But that wasn't enough for me. I needed to spread my wings and fly. Unfortunately, I had crashed and burned instead. Now, here I was, back where we had started, wondering why I had left home at all.

It all made sense why he was here plowing our driveway on the holiday—he wasn't just working—he had nowhere else to go.

Idle chitchat continued on for the rest of dinner, with Billy and me trading glances every now and again. We weren't about to catch up on almost a decade of life right at the holiday table in front of everyone. I figured after a few glasses of wine, I'd start some kind of conversation with him, although I wasn't sure what I'd say. Apologizing for breaking his heart wasn't a good opener, but I didn't have much else.

As we washed our last dish in the sink, and the boys tasted whiskey by the fire, the doorbell rang.

Unusual. First there had been a knock on the door and now the doorbell was ringing. I had no idea who it could be this time, but I figured uninvited guests were the theme this Christmas Eve, and I was going to embrace it.

I hurried to answer the door. After inhaling a deep breath, I flung the front door open wide with reckless abandon. I was ready for our holiday's next surprise.

As soon as I locked eyes with our uninvited guest, I regretted it.

My heart sank, my knees went weak and I nearly passed out. Only this time, it wasn't chemistry that had its hold on me. It was unadulterated fear.

CHAPTER FOUR

JAKE STOOD ON the doorstep of the Montgomery home and peered into the decorated bay window. Through it, he caught a glimpse of his beautiful Amelia. Her long, light-brown hair shimmered from the glow of the holiday lights. Even though her face wasn't visible, if he closed his eyes he could envision it so clearly. Her sparkling hazel eyes and voluminous eyelashes never ceased to captivate him. Amelia was perfect and that was precisely why she belonged to him.

He stomped his feet until the snow fell off of his boots. The drive to Shady Knolls had been treacherous and exhausting, and had taken much longer than he had expected. The snow was coming down much heavier than any weatherman had reported during his entire drive. *Typical meteorologists—they couldn't predict a wave coming onto shore.*

The crappy car he had driven from the city hadn't helped at all. If circumstances were different, he would have taken his luxury SUV for the road trip, but he couldn't take a chance on the car being linked to him. Worse yet, once he was on the road, Jake hadn't trusted himself to drink as much as he would have liked, which meant he was stone cold sober. He planned to make up for it later, and in a big way.

Jake didn't take any chances. He wanted to arrive alive, after all. Even if the holiday might not turn out the same way for everyone else.

He brushed the last of the snowflakes off and rang the doorbell.

The front door flung open. It was magical, just as he had imagined. There stood the love of his life, only her mouth was agape, her eyes wide. Amelia looked terrified, and Jake wasn't sure if this pleased him or upset him.

"Merry Christmas, my love." Jake stretched out his arm to hand Amelia the bouquet of red roses, but she stood there, dumbfounded.

Amelia's mother, Caroline, hovered closely behind her daughter. "Oh, Jake, you made it." She reached past Amelia to take the flowers from him. "We'll get these in water right away."

He waited there, respectfully, until he was invited into the house, like the vampire living inside of him.

Caroline must have sensed this because she said, "Come inside, grab a drink. The boys are in the living room."

Jake kissed Amelia on the cheek and made his way into the house to greet the family. Amelia shut the door and stood there for a moment, before she followed behind him. It was as if she was waiting for the perfect moment to say what was really on her mind.

After Jake delivered the Irish whiskey, he settled into the couch with Matthew and Richard. Amelia found a place to sit nearby, but not next to him.

She smiled through gritted teeth. "We need to talk."

Jake acted as if he belonged there and it was any other holiday. Originally, he hadn't been sure what kind of welcome he was going to get: either one of rage and disbelief, or warm open arms. Since he had gotten the latter, he knew he had the upper hand.

Obviously, Amelia hadn't told anyone she had broken up with him. Therefore, in his mind, all was still right in the world. They were, as he assumed, back together. Engaged again. *One day at a time*, he thought. He would use this small win to his advantage. Jake planned to have Amelia back on his terms entirely.

"Of course. Give me a few minutes to catch my breath. It's been a long and trying drive."

Amelia nervously spun her diamond around her finger, but Jake blew it off. He wasn't going to do anything unless provoked, which was how it always happened. Amelia should have known that about him by now. He was pleased, however, to notice she hadn't taken off the rock he had given her months ago. The diamond still meant something to her, exactly as he suspected.

"Here you go, Sir." Amelia's father, Richard handed Jake a glass of some unknown whiskey on the rocks.

"Ah, this is where it is at." Jake tried to be clever but it was clear he had never mastered the proper inflection and usage of slang talk. He took a tiny sip of what he assumed was cheap liquor, all the while smiling through the disgusting taste. "Excellent choice." *Liar, liar, your house might be on fire later...we'll have to see how the night goes.*

While stuck in a torturous conversation with Matthew and Kate about how *they* were pregnant—a concept that made no sense to Jake since Kate was the only one who would actually carry and deliver the child—he spotted a man he didn't recognize out of the corner of his eye.

His concentration rapidly declined until his gaze fixated on the man. He was practically dressed in rags, with dirty jeans, construction boots, and a plaid flannel jacket. From his estimation, the man talking to Caroline was homeless and they had taken him in for the holiday. The pressure on Jake's chest released for a moment with the thought.

Something kept niggling at Jake. Something deep inside was telling him the man in their house was much more than a stranger to the Montgomery family. Maybe it was the warmth in Caroline's expression, or the way he leaned against the countertop, as if relaxed and at home. It was as though he had stood in Caroline's kitchen hundreds of times talking to Amelia's mother like she were his own.

Jake's gut instinct infuriated him. It was about time he learned exactly who the strange man was standing in his in-laws' kitchen.

He interrupted Matthew and told him he would be right back.

Amelia reacted. "Where are you going?"

"To meet your friend." Jake marched with purpose right up to the man, with Amelia fast on his heels.

Interrupting the conversation, Caroline was taken aback. "Oh, Jake, I'm so sorry. I didn't mean to be rude."

"Not at all," Jake said. He offered the man his hand. "I'm Jake, Amelia's fiancé. Whom do I have the pleasure of meeting?"

The man's grip was tight, flexing as he shook Jake's hand. "Billy Campbell, an old family friend."

"That's funny, Amelia never mentioned you."

Billy's expression never changed. "I'm not surprised. We broke up a long time ago."

Fury encapsulated Jake, and he could barely stop himself from ripping the man's throat out with his own two hands right then and there on the spot. Before he had a chance to speak another word, Amelia's soft touch soothed him, even if only temporarily.

"Let's go sit by the fire, Jake. We're going to do gifts soon." Amelia hooked her arm with his, practically dragging him into the living room.

Before they made it to the couch, he whispered in her ear. "Get him out of here, or you'll witness a rage in me like you've never encountered before."

Amelia quivered, and then spoke in a muted tone. "Relax. There's nothing to freak out about. He's here to plow the driveway. I'm trying to protect my family from our relationship issues as long as I can. Don't make a scene and screw it up, okay?"

Jake appreciated her resolve, but he had no intention of listening to her. "Fine."

They went through the process of exchanging gifts and all the while, Jake was focused with laser precision on the way Billy and Amelia traded secretive glances. When the present ritual was over, Jake decided it was time to take matters into his own hands, regardless of what Amelia wanted. None of this was about Amelia anyway; it was about what Jake wanted. And Jake always got what he wanted.

Later on, when Amelia was in the kitchen with Caroline preparing dessert, Billy went outside. Jake followed inconspicuously behind.

Billy was resting comfortably against the railing on the front porch when he lit up a cigarette. Jake hated Billy's ease, his contentment. It was as if Billy belonged there and Jake was the outsider. It infuriated him.

He positioned himself directly in front of Amelia's ex-boyfriend. Their eyes met. Billy showed no fear—not a care in the world. He exhaled his smoke right into Jake's face. Jake was determined to fix Billy's attitude problem.

Jake unbuttoned his sports coat until the forty-five strapped beneath it was exposed. Billy looked at him in confusion and Jake was pleased. He said nothing in response. Instead, he pulled the gun out of its shoulder holster and pointed it directly at Billy.

CHAPTER FIVE

I SEARCHED THE cabinets for the cake plates, and the courage to tell my mother the truth before it was too late. There was no way I could go on with the charade Jake had been playing with Billy all night long. Wondering how Jake planned to punish Billy wasn't only incredibly uncomfortable. It was nerve-wracking.

I had noticed the same demon in Jake's eyes before. The only outcome of his rage on fire was pure destruction. Our saving grace was that we were celebrating Christmas, and he was obviously hoping to reconcile with me, even though it was never going to happen.

I might be able to appease him for the night, but I had no faith in Jake controlling himself long enough to avoid an all out disaster when it came to Billy.

I had no choice. I had to tell my family the truth.

That's when I heard the front door close, twice. I glanced into the living room. Both Billy and Jake were gone. My frantic heart was beating out of my chest, so loudly it sounded in my ears.

With silent discretion, I walked into the living room and peered out the window. That's when I saw it.

Jake was pointing a gun at Billy.

I burst outside in a flash and screamed. "Jake, what are you doing? Put the gun down!"

Jake turned around, an evil growing in his eyes and in his grin. "Relax. I was showing Billy the latest addition to my collection. He's a gun guy." Jake pointed to Billy's pickup in the driveway with a shotgun racked in the cab.

My hands shook as I released a breath, untrusting of Jake but unsure of how to react. I looked to Billy for direction.

"It's cool, Amelia." Billy's eyes darted from Jake and back to me as if to say, *I got this. He may be an asshole, but he's not going to scare me.*

"You heard him. He said it's cool. We're good. We'll be in soon. Now, go on inside." Jake turned back around and started to make idle conversation with Billy.

I played along. "Got it."

The moment I shut the door, Jake's threats would undoubtedly ensue. I went back inside the house to find my whole family in the living room staring at me.

"What's wrong with you?" It was clear my dad was seeing red, as if I'd ruined the holiday by being ridiculous.

"Let them be, Amelia. Boys will be boys. They need to work it out. It's a power thing. Come on, finish helping me in the kitchen." My mom wiped her hands on her apron and went back to getting the desserts out.

Kate looked at me with worried eyes. "Are you sure you're okay?"

I nodded.

"I'll help Mom. You do what you need to do, all right?" Kate turned and walked away.

I wasn't sure what I needed to do exactly, but I instinctively knew Matt would be involved. I grabbed my brother's arm and pulled him aside. "Listen to me, but don't make a fuss."

Matt scrunched his face in confusion. "You're scaring me, Mel. What's up?"

I whispered the truth. "Jake's certifiable. We broke up two days ago and he's been stalking me ever since. He came here uninvited. I didn't want to say anything because I didn't want to upset anyone. I have to be honest with you—Jake isn't afraid to hurt someone, even all of us. He's tried to push me around before. I've bared witness to what he's capable of doing. When I walked out there a moment ago, he was pointing a gun at Billy. Not showing him a gun, but pointing a gun at him. Do you understand what I'm saying?"

Matt nodded. "Should we call the police?"

I shuffled a bit, not knowing the answer to his question. "Possibly at some point, yes. But, I don't want to overreact yet. At the very least, Jake needs to leave and not come back. I don't trust him being here, especially not with Billy. If anything happens to set him off, he's liable to snap. And then we're all screwed."

Matt rubbed his forehead. "Leave it to me. I'll handle this. In the meantime, keep Jake happy until we can figure out a way to get him out of here. For good."

"Fine. But don't do anything stupid or predictable. Jake is brilliant and crazy, so if he thinks you or anyone else is onto the truth, he'll lose it, and that's not something any of us wants to experience."

"Understood." Matt walked me back to the kitchen. "Go play nice and I'll come up with the plan. Please tell Mom that Jake needs to leave but doesn't want to seem like a jerk.

We all need to stage a cancellation of Christmas Eve and then Jake will be able to leave without any guilt."

"Done." I kissed Matt on the cheek. "Thank you."

"Love you. You're safe here, Mel. Always will be."

Matt pulled Dad aside. He was bringing him up to date. It would take everything my father had in him not to react, but he had to know the truth. He was the only one with the keys to unlock the weapons. More than any of us, he needed to be fully aware and on our side should mayhem break out.

I talked to Mom and Kate. We were all on the same page. The plan was in motion.

I opened the front door and the rush of cold hit me, more so in my bones than my flesh. Something deep down stirred.

Billy was gone.

Jake was in the rocking chair, moving it back and forth sipping his whiskey as if it was any other holiday. There was no gun in sight.

My stomach dropped.

I wanted to ask where Billy was, but it would only enrage Jake. Instead, I focused on faking semi-reconciliation. He needed to let his guard down and, hopefully, go along with the rest of the night.

I took a deep breath, put on my most remorseful face and walked over to the psycho on my porch. "I apologize. I acted like such a fool."

"Forgiven." Jake reached out his hand and pulled me down on his lap.

I summoned the courage to not resist, and fell into him. "I really am grateful you came to celebrate with us."

"I was certain my visit would please you." Jake fingered my hair gently a few times, and then grabbed a tight hold of it, yanking my head back. He whispered in my ear. "Don't ever betray me like that again. Next time, you won't have an opportunity to be sorry." Then he released his grip on me.

My heart pounded uncontrollably. "Let's go inside for some dessert."

"Let's." Jake lifted me up to standing and then followed me inside the house.

CHAPTER SIX

AFTER DESSERT ENDED, Jake and Amelia made their way to the roaring fireplace. The family was settling down for the evening. Given how the holiday had gone up until that point, Jake assumed he would be staying overnight. Especially since he and Amelia were officially back together. Plan A, as he hoped, was in effect. Christmas morning had never looked so good.

He was pleased Amelia had reconsidered their brief separation, but it hardly surprised him. What woman in their right mind would trade a striking, well-to-do fiancé in exchange for a has-been with dirt under his nails? Not his Amelia, that's for sure. She was a class act, no matter where she had come from. He had elevated her status over the course of their relationship, training her well for her role as his wife, and he wasn't about to let go of her without a battle. Besides, she knew better. Her only future was wrapped tightly in Jake's arms and under his control.

In the middle of the Christmas movie marathon Jake was enduring like a champ, Kate rushed into the living room and interrupted. "Amelia, I need you in here."

Amelia sprung from the couch. "I'm coming."

Richard straightened. "Is everything all right in there?" He joined the women attending to Caroline.

Matthew peeked his head into the kitchen. "Looks like Mom isn't feeling well again."

Jake rolled his eyes and went back to sipping on his two-hundred-dollar whiskey. The flask he had stashed in his jacket sure came in handy. The one thing he had loved about his dysfunctional, upper-class family—when they were still around—was that there was no unnecessary drama. Here, it was a different story. There was always something going on that needed attention. People couldn't gather themselves enough to act proper for a few measly days of the year—the important days, nonetheless. If they wanted to go back to drinking vodka for breakfast and smacking around their wives on December 26 like his family had always done, then so be it. On certain days, you suited up and you showed up, because if it wasn't for pretending to be the person you weren't, we would all be walking around in bathrobes smelling like yesterday's trash. Nobody wanted to see the real person you were; they wanted an image of the person they expected. Jake was an image. The Montgomery family was about to find out who the real monster underneath Jake's image was, and they would be sorry.

Matthew turned to Jake. "She hasn't been herself lately. Not sure what's going on. You know my family, they're always overreacting to one thing or another."

Jake nodded. "I'm staying out of their way."

"Good call."

Kate called to her husband. "Hey, she's really sick this time. We may need to take her to the hospital."

Matthew traded places with Amelia, who looked worried.

"I think the party's over. Mom feels terribly guilty about ruining the holiday."

As she should. "Well, this is about as hard as I party. Don't mind me."

Amelia bit her lip. "That's the thing, Jake, she won't say it, but I will. I think you should go."

Jake raised his eyebrows. "I'm not going anywhere. It's horrendous out there. My truck is in the shop. I had to use a loaner piece of garbage." He leaned into her. "Amelia, darling, it's simply unsafe for me to ride all the way back to New York in these conditions." He tipped his head to the window and raised his glass. "I've been drinking. You know what they say, don't drink and drive. It's unlawful." He was perfectly capable of driving under the influence; however, he had no intention of leaving.

"I'm not asking you." Amelia stood over him, her expression begging him to go quietly.

For once, Jake recognized putting up a fight wasn't going to work to his benefit. He would have to find a way to let her believe he was leaving on her terms. He hoped her reaction wasn't an indication of Plan B being forced into action, but Amelia would be the one to determine it.

"All right." He grabbed her hand. "Then you will come with me."

The tension in her grasp told him she had no desire to do so, and he couldn't figure out if it was because of her mother being sick, or because of him.

"You know I can't leave her," Amelia said, but this time, her smile looked forced.

Jake was well aware of what he had to do. "Understood." He gathered his things and headed to the door. "I'll be back in the morning." He leaned in to kiss her, but she pulled away.

"No, you won't, Jake. I'm sorry, but I need to be with my family...alone." Amelia was overreacting. She was falling right back into her dramatic and attention-seeking ways.

Jake stared her down for a brief second to get his point across. "I'm your family." He lifted her hand and squeezed her ring finger. "Or, did you forget that's what it means when you accept a man's marriage proposal?"

The fear returned to her eyes for the briefest of moments. She tried to recover but failed. Jake slowly unraveled the truth and it hit him like an iron fist. Amelia had been bluffing the whole time. He couldn't decipher if Caroline was truly sick, or if it was a ploy to get rid of him. Either way, he would soon find out and if he were right, there would be more than hell to pay.

"I need a few days, okay? I want to make sure she's better." Amelia kissed him on the cheek but it left him cold. "Drive safely. Let me know when you get home."

He acquiesced, temporarily. "Understood." Jake kissed her hard this time, showing both his jaded love for her and his fierce anger. "Give your family my regards." He quietly turned and sauntered away.

Jake positioned his car in the perfect location on Winter Road—far enough away from Amelia's house to be hidden, but close enough to watch everything going on, even more so with his high-powered binoculars.

A half-hour after he had begun his stakeout, two odd things happened. First, it occurred to him no one had left the Montgomery household to take Caroline to the hospital or otherwise. Second, it wasn't an ambulance pulling into their driveway, but Billy Campbell's pickup.

Jake dropped his binoculars. Emotions he couldn't

reconcile raged inside of him creating a kaleidoscope of fury, jealousy, and desire. He threw open the car door and stomped to the trunk. He traded his overnight attire for weaponry, and resolved from that point forward to initiate Plan B.

CHAPTER SEVEN

MY CELL PHONE buzzed with a text message from Jake saying he was halfway home and not to worry. I was far from worried. Relieved was more like it. Especially since Billy had come back. He said he had left so he wouldn't cause any problems. Apparently when I spoke to Matt, he told Billy the truth. Once Billy was certain Jake was gone, he returned.

The whole family was relieved. They all strongly encouraged me to file a restraining order against Jake right after the holidays, although the idea of it set my nerves on edge. It would be a drastic move for me, and an embarrassing one for Jake, but I couldn't let him get away with his behavior. Pissing Jake off wasn't something one did lightly. And taking legal action against him also meant taking a risk with my life. In the end, I was the only one to decide if I preferred to live in an abusive situation, or live in fear for my life. Since being in an abusive relationship was already living in fear for my life, the choice was clear. *What more do I have to lose?*

With everyone focused on the holiday again, enjoying

the Christmas tree and cheesy movies on cable, I found myself in deep conversation with Billy—the last person I had expected to be reunited with tonight, or ever again. I had broken his heart. My ego assumed he hadn't forgiven me, but apparently I was wrong.

Billy shook his head. "I can't believe this happened tonight."

"I know. What a nightmare." I looked down. "I'm so sorry we ruined your holiday." I felt terrible. I hadn't been in the man's presence in almost a decade and he had walked into the worst situation imaginable. I was humiliated.

Billy put his hand on mine. "No, Amy."

My heart jumped. He was the only person who had ever called me Amy. I was always either Mel or Amelia to the world. The sound of his voice saying aloud the name he had given me ten years ago, the one I hadn't heard since I saw him last, awoke warmth in my heart I had forgotten all about.

He nearly knocked me over with his gaze. "This—me and you—makes my holiday."

"Oh." I felt my cheeks warm. He had caught me way off guard. The selfish part of me figured Billy was referring to my relationship woes when, in fact, he was speaking straight from his heart. I guess Jake had rubbed off on me more than I had anticipated. It was even more of a reason to rid myself of him. "Yea, this, as you put it, is pretty cool."

The word *cool* made me feel like the sixteen-year old who was head over heels for him again. Suddenly, I was the same girl Billy fell in love with years ago. But we both knew I wasn't that girl anymore. And I was certain Billy Campbell would want nothing to do with the new, and not improved, real me.

"When's the big day?" Billy asked, nodding at my ring

finger. He was half-joking but his eyes held a glint of seriousness.

"It's complicated." There would be no big day anymore,
but I hadn't taken the ring off. It spoke less to how I felt
about Jake and more to whom I wanted to be with the ring
on: a fiancée, a future wife—a woman whose man loved her
so unconditionally that he asked to share his life with her. It
was the furthest truth from my reality, but it felt good to
pretend.

Billy pursed his lips. "I figured as much."

I didn't owe him an explanation, but I wanted to give
one anyway. "I want what I can't have, is all. I think that's
why it's complicated."

"Who says you can't have it?" Billy tilted his head,
waiting for a response.

A glimmer of hope rushed me, and all of a sudden, I felt
something familiar and easy. I felt *us* again, the old Billy
and Amy, our yearbook's 'Most likely to get married and
have ten kids', we once were. For a brief moment, I
wondered if it was still possible for me to have it all. I was
young enough, only twenty-five—I had the rest of my life
ahead of me. I shook away the notion. Life didn't work out
that way. I had learned that a long time ago.

"My guardian angel. She's obviously drunk and letting
me make terrible decisions. It's hopeless." I sipped the last of
my wine.

Billy took the glass from me and refilled it. Handing it
back he said, "Where there's wine, there's hope."

I almost laughed, until I considered the meaning behind
his words. Ironically, he was right. We make our own hope.
He had handed me mine tonight in more ways than one. "I
guess we'll have to wait and see what happens, won't we?"

In all seriousness, Billy took me in with his eyes. "We most certainly will."

There it was—the possibility for my life to turn on a dime in any direction I wanted, all because of a glass of wine and an unexpected guest with hope in his heart.

Deep in conversation, we hadn't noticed everyone had dozed off around us. Whether from the stress of the evening, or the booze, the house was utterly quiet except for the crackling fire and muted holiday carols being sung on the television. The twinkling lights on the tree drew me in. Tonight wasn't what I had expected at all. I couldn't have predicted it if I had tried. But every moment, the good and the bad, was exactly what I had needed.

In that moment, it was the picture-perfect Christmas Eve. Billy leaned into me slowly. I met him halfway. Just as our lips were about to touch, the house went completely dark.

CHAPTER EIGHT

JAKE KNEW MORE than a thing or two about how houses operated. Real estate moguls didn't become *moguls* without understanding the business inside and out. Grayson Enterprises, Inc. had turned into a booming business because Jake was obsessed with knowledge and control. He forced himself to learn everything there was to know about how all buildings, including homes, operated so he could sell them, and then he trained his people to do the same. With hundreds of agents working under him for the elitist clients, he was one of the most well-known commercial real-estate brokers in New York City.

Real estate had also brought him everything he valued in his life—fortune, power, and Amelia. She was also a commercial agent, but refused to work for Jake until after they married. He hadn't fought her on this. He saw it as business opportunity since she would bring all of her clients to Grayson Enterprises.

Jake used his love of real estate to plan the evening. When he had decided to sabotage the Montgomery's Christmas, the logical next steps were for him to disable the electricity and the phone lines. The blizzard-like conditions hadn't made it easy for him, but he had gotten the job done. And it looked like he had done it with precision timing as well. Billy had cornered Amelia and was making his move on her. Jake had no choice but to intervene.

Luckily, he didn't have to worry about them using their cell phones either. Jake happened to have a friend in the area, a high-profile, and highly technically savvy drug dealer who had serviced the most elite in New York City for several decades. When he had met him at a private party, he had learned the man's family was from Shady Knolls and he had recently moved back to his hometown. Since it was shortly after he and Amelia had started dating, Jake decided it was wise to stay in touch with the man, even if only for ordering pills from time to time without the inconvenience of a doctor's appointment. Jake figured he might be able to use a contact in Amelia's hometown at some point, and as it turned out, he was right.

Drug dealers were criminals and most of them would do anything for the right amount of money. His guy was no different. In this case, money wasn't an issue for Jake and hacking into the Montgomery's cell service to disable it on cue wasn't a problem for his Shady Knolls friend either.

Cutting off communications with the outside world was the first step tonight, and it had been accomplished.

Next, he would need one of two things: Amelia, or a hostage to lure Amelia. His answer would come in the form of whoever came outside first. And he was about to find out.

Jake poured the gasoline into the box full of dry kindling—twigs, leaves, and sticks. He placed the body on top of the bed he had created. Then he added more gasoline. He couldn't take any chances on it sparking, and the weather was making everything more difficult. He was running out of time. He ran to position himself behind one of the massive pine trees on the front lawn, poised to take aim or attack. His bait was set and once he drew their attention to it, he would be close enough to make his move. Jake pointed the flamethrower at the accurate height and shot his already dead target, all for effect, of course. It went up like a bonfire, causing a glow that spanned Winter Road.

Within seconds of the blaze, the Montgomery's front door burst open. There stood Matt, Amelia, and Billy. Indignation raged inside of Jake. She was shoulder to shoulder with that pathetic loser of a man. He held steady, waiting to find out how the scenario was going to play itself out. He was as nervous and excited as he had ever been, not knowing if there would be blood, tears, or both. It was exhilarating.

Jake watched as they fought over who would go outside to find out what had happened. When the decision was finally made, Matthew Montgomery ran out of the house and straight over to the giant flames, where he found a stray cat's body on fire. He shouted profanities, and then removed his sweater and tried to extinguish the fire. Before Amelia or Billy had an opportunity to help him, Jake lifted his rifle, pointed it directly at Matthew, and pulled the trigger.

Amelia's brother, the perfect bait, never had a chance. The bullet struck him and he fell to the ground. His fiancée wailed and Billy lunged out on the porch. That's when Jake began shooting at the house. He emptied rounds of the different weapons he had strapped to him like the soldier he had once been.

Jake kept shooting and didn't stop until Amelia forcefully pulled Billy back inside of the house doing precisely what Jake expected—avoiding gunfire at all costs.

By the time it all stopped and the world went quiet

again, it was much too late for anyone to reach him. Jake had already dragged an unconscious Matthew through the snow. They were well on their trek deep into the woods.

At this point, Amelia most certainly had figured out what was going on, but there would be nothing she could do to change it. Her only choice would be to go to Jake, agreeing to be with him forever—belonging to him—and they would escape it all, far, far away from Winter Road, Shady Knolls, and anywhere else familiar.

Or, one by one, each person Amelia ever loved would die.

CHAPTER NINE

I STUMBLED INTO the house and then fell backward right on top of Billy. We crashed onto the hardwood foyer. Within seconds of the gunfire halting, I sensed the rest of my family hovering over us, but the house was still fully dark.

"I'm calling the police." Dad picked up the phone, pressed a few buttons and then slammed it down. "What has he done?" He rushed over the end table and picked up his cell phone. "No service?"

I wasn't surprised and knew all of our phones would be the same way. Jake didn't take anything to chance. He always thought his plans through, and clearly this was a well thought out plan. I wanted to scream aloud that we had no phones at all, no way to call for help and that it was hopeless, but the words never came out. I was breathless from the shock of it all: Matt going down, the bullets piercing the house, but most of all, the utter crazy that I had never seen in Jake before.

Billy lifted me to standing. He proceeded to help me over to the couch, using his hands to feel his way there.

"No use," he said to my dad. "We're on our own with this bastard."

Kate looked out the window. "He's gone. Matt's gone."

She became hysterical and Mom tried to comfort her, but it was beyond her ability. Given what had happened, we were well aware of the reality: Matt was probably dead and if not, he was close to it. Either way, he was in serious trouble because Jake had him, and Jake was out of his mind.

Dad threw the phone across the room in a rage. "That's it." He rummaged through the drawers in the kitchen until he found a flashlight. When he opened the basement door, it was clear where he was headed and what was on his mind.

"Go with him," I said to Billy, and he obliged.

Minutes later, the two of them stood suited up for war. Realizing what was about to happen, I stopped them at the door. "Let me go with Billy."

My dad looked at me like I was as crazy as Jake. "Over my dead body."

"Exactly. I don't want it to come to that, Dad. Please," I paused letting my words resonate. "I'm the one Jake's after. He's doing all of this because he wants me. Let me go to him. Maybe I can talk some sense into him or, at the very least, stop him from killing all of us."

My dad stood firm. "He's already got my son. I'm not letting that psychotic bastard get my daughter, too." There were no tears in his eyes, but they were evident in his voice.

Billy chimed in. "Rich, I hate to admit it, but she's right."

Dad snapped his head toward my ex-boyfriend. "You've got to be kidding me. Now, you're siding with my daughter?"

Billy put his hand on my dad's shoulder. "No need to worry, old man. I'll take care of your little girl."

Billy waited for me to put on my coat and boots, and

then he helped with the weapons exchange. He handed me everything my dad planned to use on Jake, if needed.

"I hope you know how to use the real thing." It had been quite some time since Billy and I had simulated target practice in my backyard.

"I've been around the range a few times."

"She's the best shot I've ever seen," my dad said.

"Like I said, you have nothing to worry about." Billy opened the door, and then turned to my dad. "Take care of them. They need you."

Dad looked back over his shoulder at Mom and Kate huddled on the couch. Their heads were down in what looked like prayer. I was glad. Matt needed a world's worth of prayers right about now.

I wanted to say goodbye to them in case something happened to either of us. But it wasn't about me. I needed to bring Matt back for his wife and his baby.

"I love you, Dad. We'll bring your boy home."

My dad nodded. "Be safe out there." Then he patted Billy on the back. "Get his crazy ass."

"Done." Billy closed the door behind him.

We stood on the porch for a brief moment. "This isn't going to end well," I said.

Billy raised his eyebrow. "No, it won't. Jake's a dead man."

We headed out, using the moon as our only real light. Flashlights would draw too much attention, we decided, and the last thing we wanted to do was give Jake a heads up. He was aware we were coming, but he didn't need to know when.

It was fully dark out. There were no stars in the sky. Even though I had grown up there, the woods on my parents' property were dense, massive and terrifying at night and even more so in a storm.

We stood at their edge, deciding which path to take. At first, I had no idea where to go. That is, until an old conversation with Jake dawned on me. His memory was razor sharp and there was no way he would forget what I had said about my childhood, especially now that it was crucial he recall the location accurately.

The old shed; deep in the woods, where my dad used to go back when a man cave wasn't a *thing*. It was small and hidden and a good distance away. Dad had never wanted us to go that far as kids. It was dangerous, he had said. Perfect for us, since we loved danger. We were kids.

One bright summer's day, because we never would have gone at night, we had navigated the woodland and found it. When we had opened the doors, we understood immediately why our dad never wanted us there. The old shed had been stocked top to bottom with weaponry. A much greater supply than what Dad ever had on hand in our basement, and we had thought that was a lot of firepower.

Jake was there. It was the only place he could be, and we were in more trouble than I ever imagined.

Billy and I didn't have a choice in the matter. We had to save Matt's life.

We took off racing into the woods and never looked back.

MILITARY TRAINING HAD come in handy for Jake. He could carry a man weighing a buck eighty over his shoulder with ease. Sure, he hadn't needed to do such a thing in a long while, but his personal trainer had certainly kept him in shape for it, and he was grateful. Nightly weight lifting sessions, balanced with the occasional Pilates class, left Jake's body practically sculpted into a work of art. He was stronger and more flexible than he had ever been and book cover model worthy. Jake was in the perfect physical shape to fend off an angry mob, and mentally prepared to kill a family.

Trudging through the snow energized him. The frozen breeze on his cheeks, the sweat pouring down his brow—if he closed his eyes, he could pretend he was summiting Everest. To stand tall after torturing himself to get to the top, possibly sacrificing others along the way, would be a dream come true for Jake one day. Until such a scenario happened, the Montgomery's backyard would have to do.

Matthew's blood left a trail for Amelia, although Jake

was certain she would know exactly where to find her brother. It was the only place Amelia had ever described in detail to Jake about her home, the one visual he had to draw from.

Not only had she been proud of her story, but she had also been enamored with what she had found there. And it was all so appealing to Jake, too, being obsessed with all forms of weaponry. The shed was a place Jake wished he'd had when he was growing up. Richard's tools certainly would have come in handy for Jake back then. He could have taught his father a lesson, or three before tragedy struck. As it was, his father's lessons came by other means. Jake made sure his mother, whom he respected despite her decision to stay all those years, would finally be free of the abusive bastard. To kill someone and get away with it at such a young age, only thirteen, had set the adult Jake into motion much earlier than normal. William Grayson's death was deemed an accident, hunting to be specific. Not surprisingly, Jake's bruised and battered mother had been right by her son's side the whole time, even though she knew the truth. The case may have been long closed, but it was still alive and breathing in Jake. He never forgot the joy murdering his father brought him, both while he was committing it and afterward when he reaped the rewards of his death. Jake learned at that young age how killing someone both eliminated problems and delivered exactly what one desired. The lesson was never lost on him, and it was one he was willing to re-learn again and again.

The current state of affairs was far different. Amelia was leaps and bounds above his mother in terms of evolution. Jake had to take some credit for that, though. He had worked diligently over the past few years to mold his fiancée into the woman he wanted her to be—more of a trophy than a partner. Of course, there was a world of difference between Jake and his father. Jake demanded respect the old-fashioned way; he wasn't a dirt bag about it. Although, it seemed his actions tonight had taken things to the extreme compared to his father's inappropriate behavior, it simply wasn't the case. *Not really.* One dramatic act wasn't any worse than the years of daily abuse his father had dealt out to him and his mother. Jake felt it was better to get it all out in the open at once, to rip off the bandage, and move on. That's distinctly what Jake was doing—ripping off the bandage, no matter how bloody the open wound underneath might be.

When Jake finally reached the shed, he hated to admit to himself that he was exhausted. The wooden barn-type structure was much smaller than Amelia had described. Jake was concerned he might not be able to pull off his master plan.

He kicked the door open first, and then dropped Matthew on the ground outside. Amelia's brother stirred but was still not fully conscious. The bullet wound alone wouldn't kill him, but the blood loss might. Or hypothermia may set in—not that Jake cared either way in which Matthew died. In fact, Jake wished he had killed Matthew on the spot exactly as originally intended. But after careful consideration, Jake had come to the conclusion such an act would only enrage Amelia—not motivate her to go to Jake.

Kidnapping her seriously injured brother was much more illusory. *Was he alive? Was he dead?* It was anyone's guess. Amelia would have no choice but to take her chances in the snowy, dark woods to find them both and learn the answer.

Amelia wasn't stupid. She wouldn't be venturing out

alone, especially not under such dangerous circumstances. *Danger*. He loved the word. The sound of it, the way it made his heart beat—thump, thump, thump—the way it made him feel so...alive.

I am the danger now.

None of it would matter because by the time Amelia and, he assumed, Billy arrived at the hidden shed, Jake would be long gone. He would already be setting the bigger stage—decking the halls—preparing for his master plan to unfold. It was one Amelia would give her life to prevent.

He was certain of it.

It's what he wanted more than anything: Amelia's life, to have and to hold. Till death do they part, even if they parted tonight. He would have his Amelia's beautiful life, one way or another.

He dragged Matthew's limp body into the shed. Jake took the time he needed to perfectly position Matt for Amelia's shocking discovery.

When Jake was done, Matthew opened his eyes and moaned. Jake lifted a shovel off of the wall and brought it down on Matthew's head. He was quiet again, exactly how Jake needed him.

He spent the next few minutes ensuring his victim was displayed perfectly. When Jake was pleased with his handi-work, he left a small piece of paper sticking out of Matthew's shirt pocket. It was a handwritten note to his love, and sealed with a kiss.

Jake closed up the shed as if he had never been there. The only telltale sign was the blood-soaked snow in front of the door welcoming Billy and Amelia inside of Jake's mini house of horrors.

Jake pulled up his collar to shield himself from the blowing snow as he headed back to the house, taking an entirely different path. There, he would unleash his evil on everyone inside. Waiting for Amelia wouldn't be easy, but finally having her all to himself was going to be well worth the wait.

Without her family alive, Jake would be all she had left.

CHAPTER ELEVEN

AFTER WE WERE well on our journey, Billy and I spotted them on the ground. Tiny droplets of blood formed a trail, confirming my suspicions. Jake had taken Matt to the shed. We were on the right track.

More than that, it gave me hope that Matt's heart was still beating. Billy and I might have a shot at saving my brother after all. That is, as long as we got to him before it was too late.

When we finally arrived, we stood quiet before the shed door. I had no idea what we would find inside. The silence of it all was deafening. For a brief moment, I considered I might have had it all wrong and the trek into the woods was a trap of some kind. The pool of blood outside the door told me someone, or something, bleeding had been there. I had no idea if it was Matt or a deer, but we had to find out.

Billy and I didn't speak a word, but the look on his face said he was prepared for war. Once we readied our weapons, I took a step in front of him and reached for the door. He shoved my hand aside and gestured for me to take a few steps back.

Billy was going in first and there was no fighting him. He had promised my dad he would take care of me, which, in their "language," meant he would gladly put my life before his. I wanted to barrel over him like I had always done when I didn't get my way, but there was no point this time. He was going to try and protect me, like he always had, whether I wanted him to or not.

I struggled with whether his resolute ways still enraged me or excited me. Either way, I made the decision I would do whatever I could to protect him, and the rest of my family, too. A heart like Billy's was hard to find. I just wish I had realized that eight years ago.

Billy inched the shed door open, slowly at first and then with a forceful thrust. We both lunged into an offensive stance, ready to attack, except we had misjudged the situation entirely.

"Bastard," Billy said, kicking his way across the small space.

If my adrenaline hadn't been rushing me at full force, I might have fallen to the ground at the sight before me. Instead, I dropped my weapon and rushed to my brother.

Matt was strung up like one of my dad's dead deer after a hunting trip. His limp limbs were hung on the wall hooks, formerly meant for tools and weapons, with some kind of wire. I could tell he was breathing, barely, and had lost a lot of blood.

Panicked, I stated the obvious. "Help me get him down." Of course, Billy was already on the task at hand.

I couldn't think straight. For once in my life, the girl who had learned to shut off her heart was overcome with emotions and fear. I was losing it at a time when losing it was the worst thing I could have done.

Billy didn't search for a wire cutter for long. He understood how my dad's brain worked; they were bred from the same kind of cloth. He found it within seconds and got to work.

I held up Matt's body as best I could, leaning on a nearby workbench for support while Billy did what he needed to get Matt down. Soon enough, we were able to position my hardly conscious brother on the floor and tried to make him comfortable.

"Hang in there, buddy," Billy said.

I couldn't drum up anything valuable to say. Instead, I held his hand, and my tears.

Matt was mumbling, half in and out of consciousness. I believe he realized we were there with him, but he was probably in shock and, from the loss of blood, in bad shape.

His shirt was thoroughly blood soaked. Even at first glance, it looked like he had been shot in the chest. If it were true, my brother wouldn't be alive for much longer.

Billy opened Matt's shirt to expose his chest. It was stained crimson, but we were able to confirm Matt had not been shot in the heart. The bullet had struck him in the upper chest, closer to his shoulder and, thankfully, from what we could tell, no vital organs.

It was good news, even though Matt didn't look good at all. His color was off, a touch too pale. He wore a giant gash on his forehead as if he had been hit there, and hard. His gunshot wound needed to be attended to by doctors, not family and friends. No matter how the night went down, Matt needed to get to the hospital if he was going to have a chance to live. I had no idea how I was going to get him help, but I had to take action and fast.

"You're going to make it." Billy gritted his teeth, resolved. "We're going to get that son-of-a-bitch if it's the last thing we ever do."

I wasn't sure if he would live, and I hated to think it would be the last thing we did, but I could agree with Billy otherwise. "I'm right here, Matt. It's Mel. I'm here."

Jake wasn't going to make it out of this nightmare alive if either of us had anything to do with it. My only wish for this holiday was to have my family, including Billy, around to see Christmas morning.

Billy and I shared a moment where our eyes met, and all of a sudden we were teenagers again. He understood me almost telepathically. Billy had to find Jake. If he wasn't in the shed, there was only one place he could have gone, and he had to stop him.

"Go," I said. "Go save my family from that monster. Please, Billy. I'll stay here with Matt."

Billy leaned down, grabbed my face in his hands and kissed my forehead. "I know you can take care of yourself if he comes back. There's not much we can do for Matt until we get Jake under control. You're both much safer here than anywhere else on your property." He looked me straight in the eyes. "Don't worry, Amy. I have a plan."

I believed him. Not because I wanted to, but because he was the most honest person I had ever known. And the look in his hazel eyes told me; he would die tonight to save us.

When Billy closed the door to the shed, I exhausted all the tears I'd been holding in up until that point.

I was going to die tonight. We were all going to die tonight.

CHAPTER TWELVE

BILLY TOOK A more complicated route through the woods. He knew the property well after having practically grown up there, and more recently with his landscaping business. Jake was limited in his knowledge, although Billy had to give the psycho credit for figuring it out. He didn't want Jake to find him out there, or for Amy to catch up with him.

Amy.

He couldn't believe how beautiful she was, even after all the years they had missed together. And insanely successful—she had become exactly the woman he expected she would, with the exception of her choice in men.

The snow was coming down in sheets, heavier than it looked when he had peered outside earlier. In the short time since he had traveled to the shed and back, it seemed like inches had fallen. It was hard to walk, even harder to run, but Billy was an outdoorsman and breaking a sweat didn't bother him. What bothered him was Jake.

Billy was certain Jake had killed before, even if only in the military. He was a sociopath and likely a serial killer. It was evident in his eyes, with their cold, dark emptiness. The man may have told Amy he loved her, but he was feigning his emotions. Jake didn't know a thing about love. He only knew obsession and possession.

When Billy reached the front of the house, his truck was hardly recognizable. The storm had done some damage, with much more snow than expected falling. Not only was he covered, but also his red pickup was practically invisible under the mountains of white powder.

He imagined all the people who were likely thrilled with a heavy snowstorm on Christmas Eve. All of those families safe in their homes cozied up by the fire, the parents reading holiday stories to their kids, watching festive shows on television. Everyone else was celebrating the holiday the way they should be, and the way the Montgomery family deserved to celebrate. Yet, here he was, with Amy and her family, fighting for their lives.

The darkness was a blessing for Billy. Without any light shining outside, he had a better chance of going unseen. He was certain Jake was watching and waiting for him to come back to the house. It was all a game for Jake, the back and forth—the chase. The bastard wanted a hunt. Little did he know that he was about to become the hunted.

Billy got down on the ground and crawled the rest of the way to his truck. It would be harder for Jake to locate him on the ground, especially on the outside of the driveway, which is where he always parked when his plow was attached.

Billy entered the vehicle from the passenger's side, slowly opening the door enough to fit his oversized body into the cab. He barely made any noise and caused minimal movement. Unless Jake was staring out the front window, actively looking for him, Jake wouldn't have been able to spot Billy.

He tuned his state-of-the-art CB radio to Channel 9. There was static, but he tried his luck anyway. "Breaker, breaker. Anyone out there have your ears on? Campbell Soup here. I need a 10-38 and 10-200 at 36 Winter Road, Shady Knolls. Send your Band Aid Buggy and a Full Grown Bear or County Mounty pronto."

"Campbell Soup. Here's a County Mounty. It's Bullet Boy. What's going on over there? Is the Montgomery family okay?" Robbie Dodson, aka CB handle Bullet Boy, for his stellar marksmanship, was a high school friend as well as a local Shady Knolls police officer.

"The Montgomery house is under siege. Some asshole from New York, Jake, lost his mind on Amy. Matt's been shot and everyone else is being held hostage. I'm about to go in and try to disable him, but I can't do this alone. Get over here and send back up."

"I'm on it, Billy. No time to waste. You be careful in there. Over and out." Robbie hung up.

Billy turned the CB off. At least help was on the way. Although if the Shady Knolls Police Department didn't use their minds along with their excessive force, everyone would end up dead.

Billy had learned, in his short-lived time in Jake's presence, that he was a master manipulator, an astute planner, and as crazy as they came. Billy wasn't sure if he had just helped the situation or signed all of their death certificates. Either way, he had to do his part. And like Robbie said, there was no time to waste.

Billy was already armed, but he didn't want to take any chances. He grabbed a few more items from the truck, including his vest with unending hiding places, shoving whatever he could into each concealed pocket. Lastly, he snatched his prized possession—a forty-five semi-automatic handgun. He had to go in with a weapon that was both easily maneuverable and incredibly powerful.

He didn't think about using it, he couldn't. Billy was a tough guy on the outside, but as sensitive as they came on the inside. He had never considered himself a killer, not even at the present time. But if he were forced to take a life in order to save the ones he treasured, Amelia and her family, he would pull the trigger again and again, and have no regrets.

Billy exited the truck as quietly as he had entered, and then he headed back to the house. He was as armed and dangerous as Jake, and it felt downright phenomenal.

Billy flung open the Montgomery's front door in one fell swoop. His arms were raised and he was ready to take down Jake. He was prepared for war.

CHAPTER THIRTEEN

JAKE WAS PROUD of himself. He had made it back to the house in record time. Peering through the kitchen window he saw variations of shadows, slight movement of one or two people inside.

He didn't have much time to prepare the Montgomery family for Amelia and Billy; they would be back before long. She was smart and he was strong—two more difficult targets than what stood before him.

No worries for Jake though, he worked fast. He had hoisted and tied up Matt in no time. It was the hunt Jake loved the most. Any version of cat and mouse he had the opportunity to play, he did. It was his favorite kind of game. A versatile form of entertainment, Jake had been taking part in it for quite some time. It all originated in the military, both in training and when he was in the field overseas. Of course, it was much more advanced than what he had created of late, but thoroughly as strategic.

Stalking and tracking Amelia, planning his next move in anticipation of her next move, was all in an effort to control the outcome and win. Winning was Jake's style. He was always three steps ahead of his opponent. That's why, when it came to games, Jake never lost. He wasn't a loser. He was a winner. And tonight would be no different.

He cracked their back door open and entered silently. Jake was a master at working in the dark. Being caught off guard would be the least of Richard, Caroline, and Kate's problems. Jake had to make sure that if he injured them, it was without serious harm, which wouldn't be easy. Richard had a cardiac condition, Caroline looked like she had some kind of serious illness, and Kate was pregnant. Unless he wanted them dead before Amelia arrived, he needed to be strategic about how he manhandled them. Jake had a way of letting his rage get the better of him.

Jake peeked around the wall between the rooms. Caroline and Kate were having a conversation, commiserating about Matt when they should have been worrying about what could happen to them. Richard was attempting to worry for all of them, as he paced behind the couch, mumbling to himself something about *getting that bastard*.

Unfortunately, he didn't have a chance.

Jake waited until Richard's back was turned and lunged at him. He hooked the rope around his neck from behind and took him down to the floor. Caroline and Kate screamed as if they were being attacked. Caroline came at Jake from the side, while Richard struggled beneath his grasp.

Jake did the logical thing. He pointed the gun at Richards's head and calmed them both down in seconds. "You watched me shoot Matthew. Clearly, I'm comfortable pulling the trigger of a gun. Don't tempt me."

Caroline backed up slowly with her hands up as if Jake was pointing the gun at her. "Don't hurt him. We'll back off."

She grabbed Kate's hand and pulled her deeper into the room, away from Jake and Richard.

"What the hell is wrong with you?" Kate's voice swirled with tears and anger.

Jake walked slowly toward Kate. "You should ask Amelia what's wrong with her." He ripped a syringe from his pocket and thrust it into Kate. She stumbled back a few steps until she fell onto the couch. Caroline screamed. Richard shuffled behind him. Jake was running out of time. He had to move fast.

With another syringe, he pierced Caroline's upper arm in one swift motion. She did much the same, slumping next to Kate.

When Jake turned around, Richard was opposite him. He was wielding an umbrella and he charged Jake with it. He grabbed hold of the tip and he pulled until it twisted Richard's arm in an unnatural position. Richard dropped the umbrella and Jake was on top of the man, knocking him over until he hit the ground hard. Jake dragged Richard back until he was up against the wall bordering the stairs.

Jake was running out of time. He needed to make sure Richard wouldn't struggle or attempt to fight back. Jake looked around to ensure Caroline and Kate weren't mobile. He pushed Richard's shirt up until his bicep was exposed.

"What are you doing?" Richard stirred, tried to pull away from Jake.

"Shut up, old man," Jake nodded toward the women, "or you'll regret it."

Amelia's father bristled. His face was resolute, as if he understood he had no choice but to play Jake's game through to the end. But, Richard's eyes darting to the door said it wasn't his first choice. He was waiting for rescue that would never come.

Jake stuck the needle into Richard's arm and pressed the sedative into his flesh. Before long, he slumped a bit and relaxed like Caroline and Kate. They weren't asleep, but they weren't entirely awake either. Jake liked to call it the *half-in/half-out* syndrome.

With three of his victims readied, he worked on setting the stage.

The foyer chandelier placement was perfect for Jake's plan with Richard. He unzipped his backpack and took out the tools he needed. Standing on the stairs and leaning slightly, Jake reached the fixture by a hair's breadth. With heavy-duty screws, he drilled through the ceiling medallion and, luckily, hit a beam. He attached the rope first. Then he tested its strength by hanging from it and swinging off the ground. He had to make sure the medallion was secure. It needed to hold Richard's weight.

When he was convinced it was secure, Jake lifted Richard into a sitting position in a nearby chair. Jake looped the remainder of the rope secured on the medallion around Richard's neck, ready for an old-fashioned hanging. He gagged him with a holiday napkin, using duct tape to secure it inside of his mouth.

Jake repeated the same process with Caroline and Kate, securing their nooses to the ceiling beams.

When the time was right, Jake would force each of them to stand, leaving their fate in their balance.

As if perfect timing, the front door flung open. Billy marched inside the house, his gun raised. Richard moaned aloud to warn Billy of what was behind him. Billy stopped in his tracks and it was more than enough time for an attack.

Jake shot out from behind the front door. Billy must have heard the movement because he turned around. Jake grabbed Billy's collar and pulled him down. When he fell on top of Jake, Billy's neck was exposed. Jake was about to shove the needle into the bare flesh when Billy shifted slightly. They wrestled around until he flipped over and found an advantage point, right on top of Jake. Billy squeezed until the syringe flew out of Jake's hand and landed somewhere across the room.

Billy had the gun pointed at Jake's temple, when Jake found a rage within he had forgotten still existed. Every past wrong in his life rose to the surface of his mind. He wrestled with Billy as if he were his father come back to life, with everything he had inside of him. Billy might have been stronger, but Jake had manipulation on his mind. And it was set on murder.

Jake knocked the gun out of Billy's hand. Billy struggled to retrieve it, but Jake got the upper hand. He shoved an elbow into Billy's throat while he stretched to grab the gun. It was a short distance from his hand, but far enough away that he couldn't reach it. Jake would have to release Billy for a brief moment to get the gun, and then take his chances on getting control again.

He had no choice. Billy was Jake's biggest threat. He had to shoot him. He would take care of the rest of the family when Amelia arrived.

He released his hold on Billy and dove for the gun. Jake got the weapon, but when he turned around to use it, Billy was gone.

CHAPTER FOURTEEN

ALTHOUGH MATT WAS fading fast, I had to leave him. If I tried to bring him with me, he would only slow me down and there was no time to waste. Jake was a killer and my family's lives were at risk. Billy was on a mission and he had gotten a head start. I was afraid if I had told him my plan, he would have tried to stop me. Besides, he would never think I'd leave Matt behind.

Looking at him, lying there all pale and weak, broke my heart. Truth was, I couldn't help him until I got help and it wasn't going to happen stuck in the shed in the woods.

I made sure there was pressure on his wound. Matt was propped upright enough to prevent him from choking if he vomited. It was the best I could do. I kissed him on the forehead.

"Love you, Matty. I'll be right back for you. Hang in there."

Matt blinked back a few tears. "I'm good." His voice was weak, but he was strong, always had been. He had to survive, and I had to believe he would. It was the only way I could leave him.

I closed the door of the shed and took off running. I sprinted as fast as I could in the snow. My feet numbed more with each step; the ice making its way into my shoes that were never meant for tromping through the snow.

My mind was focused, as sharp as any blade. There was no fear, no anger—nothing on my mind but sheer determination. All I wanted was to make it to the house in one piece. I would deal with whatever Jake had in store for me afterward.

My heart raced. It pounded against my ribcage like it was struggling to escape somehow. I took in as much oxygen as I could but the air was thin. Running hurt, from my chest to my toes. Everything was painful.

I decided I was willing to suffer for them, my family. No one should have to endure Jake's wrath. I had made my decision. I was the one who had brought Jake into our world, and I would be the one to get him out. Only me and no one else.

My exhaled breath created a cloud that looked like smoke. I wished I was relaxed enough to have a cigarette instead of plowing through my parents' woods on Winter Road, headed for certain disaster.

It was all about us—Jake and me. We were the most broken couple, the most messed up two people that had ever come together. I had caused all of this. I was to blame and it was my job to fix everything and make it right again.

I rounded the corner to the house and pulled up short. It was utterly silent. A terrible sign, one I wasn't sure I was prepared to face. I had no idea what I was walking into, but I had to go in. Hands up, heart out, surrendering.

Before I reached the porch, I spotted movement from the corner of my eye. I turned my head, expecting to find Jake. Instead, it was Billy.

He put his finger over his mouth, signaling me to be quiet. I pulled back a few feet until I was hidden on the side of the house, out of view from whoever was inside, so we could communicate without words. I pointed to the house, indicating my plan was to go inside. Billy didn't fight me. He must have figured out I would be the only one with any chance to get through to Jake, who had clearly lost his mind.

I smiled. Billy believed in me, and it meant more to me than anything. He made the universal gesture for crazy, and I knew he meant Jake. Then he mouthed for me to be careful.

I raised my shoulders and put my palms out in question of what he was doing. He made a circular motion above his head with his hand, signaling the police were on their way. I pointed to the woods. Billy was well aware Matt needed urgent care, but I wanted to press the point to ensure Matt would be taken care of first. Billy told me he understood by making the thumbs up sign.

It amazed me how Billy and I were able to communicate more effectively using made-up sign language in the dark after nearly a decade than Jake and I ever had with real words and daily interaction.

I wasn't going to worry. It relieved me to know Billy had a plan. I wasn't in this nightmare alone.

Then I did what I came there to do...I made my way up to the front door. Although I was relieved help was on the way at some point, I realized it might take some time. Everything was slower in Shady Knolls, which was normally fine by me. Except when you needed them to be lightning fast, like now. I had to take matters into my own hands in the meantime. My immediate goal was to calm Jake down long enough to prevent him from killing anyone before Matt was rescued and the cops, hopefully, infiltrated the house.

I didn't put it past Jake to massacre all of us and escape unscathed.

With a deep breath, I placed my hand on the front door handle. I had no idea if my plan would work, but it was all I had. I said a little prayer and cracked the door open.

At first, all I saw was darkness. When I pushed the door open further and entered the house, the worst scenario, one I couldn't have imagined if I had tried, took shape before my eyes.

Directly in front of me was my father. His eyes were full of tears at the sight of me. He stood off-balance on a kitchen chair in the foyer. There was a noose tied around his neck and it was attached to the ceiling. One wrong move and the chair would come out from under him. His neck would be broken in an instant. He moaned and it broke my heart.

I gasped, but before I could let out the air, my eyes caught sight of my mom and Kate. They looked terrified, strung up in the same way as my dad. They sounded like they were crying beneath their gags.

It took everything in my power not to start releasing each one of them. But I knew it was all a trap. One wrong move on my part, and all of us would be dead.

As I stepped further into the room, I put my hand up to let them know to be quiet. I didn't want Jake to know I was there, especially if he was waiting for a reaction. Scanning my family, I saw all of their eyes grow wide.

The front door slammed behind me and unseen arms attacked me, dragging me across the room. I screamed. The hand I had held countless times, the hand I believed I once loved, snuffed out my voice. I tried to bite him, but it was impossible. I kicked wildly as he pulled me into the kitchen.

Before I had a chance to react, I felt a pinch in my neck.

The bastard was drugging me. I expected to pass out, but I didn't. Instead, I became a foggier version of myself, one that couldn't think clearly, or move fluidly, but was able to function.

It all made sense. He had drugged my family to prevent them from fighting back. If they moved, they were dead. Either Jake hadn't encountered Billy yet, or he had escaped. I wasn't sure but from the looks of him, he was perfectly fine.

Jake used the rope on me, but not like he had with the others. He didn't put a noose around my neck and string me up. Instead, he tied me to the armchair so I wouldn't move.

"What are you doing?" The question sounded like one long, slurred and undecipherable word.

Jake kneeled down in front of me. "I'm getting you back, my love. One way or another, you will belong to me."

"You can have me. You don't need to hurt my family. Let them go."

He laughed, almost hysterically. "That's where you're wrong, Amelia. The only way you will belong to me, and for good, is if there's no one in this world left for you."

I was about to scream, "No" and plead with him, when he grabbed a holiday napkin from the table and shoved it in my mouth. I tried to spit it out, but he wrapped duct tape around my head securing it.

My anxiety raged inside of me. I was certain I couldn't breathe, but my nostrils were free. I took a deep sniff of air and once it reached my lungs, I relaxed.

Jake massaged my shoulders. "There, there, love. It will all be over soon."

He pushed the chair, with me in it, until I was in the living room with the rest of my family.

We were all going to die. Worse, Jake was going to make me watch him murder my family one by one, and there was nothing I could do about it.

CHAPTER FIFTEEN

THE MOMENT AMY entered the house, Billy took off running. She was entering the gates to Hell, but he couldn't help her without a team of people behind him. In reality, Amy was the only person Jake would keep alive, at least until the very end. She had time to live, and as much as he cared for her family, Amy was his top priority—always had been and always would be.

Billy had never stopped loving her, not even when she left him to pursue her dreams in the big city. He used to wonder if she had gotten all she wanted out of life, because it would have made losing her worth it.

Now he knew the truth. If they all survived this tragedy, he planned on spending the rest of his life showing Amy exactly how she deserved to be treated. He would prove to her what real love was, all over again.

Billy barreled down the steep driveway until he reached Winter Road. There was only one logical way they would enter, from the East where Main Street intersected with Winter Road.

He banked left and kept running, even though it wasn't easy. The snow, ice and slush had made it nearly impossible. Slipping and sliding along, he managed to stay on course. He had to intercept the ambulance and barrage of cop cars before the sight and sound of them set Jake on edge. They had to attack quietly, or all hell would absolutely break loose and there would be no survivors.

Winter Road was utterly silent, whether from the storm or the holiday. He was surprised no one had arrived yet. It had seemed like forever since he had spoken to Robbie. Certainly, he had taken Billy seriously. He prayed as much, because Robbie was their only hope. Matt couldn't wait much longer without medical care, and Jake had already inflicted harm on the others. Whatever else was going on inside that house wasn't good.

Billy reached the end of Winter Road where it met Main Street and saw all of the lights flashing. He stood in the middle of the street waving his hands like some crazy person. Thank goodness the officer driving the first car was Robbie. He slammed on his brakes, put the car in park and got out. He gestured to the cop cars and ambulance to follow suit.

"What's the hold up?" Robbie threw his hands up in frustration.

"I could ask you the same thing."

"We're here, aren't we? But, tell me...why the hell are you standing in the middle of the road blocking our way?"

"To stop you from going to the Montgomery's house with your guns blazing."

Robbie wore a confused look. "Isn't this what you wanted from us? Don't waste our time with bullshit, Bill. We all have families we'd rather be spending tonight with instead of risking our lives out here with some wanna-be psycho."

Billy shook his head. "No, Robbie, you're misunderstanding me. I want all of you at the house, but not with your guns blazing. Jake's no wanna-be. He's the real deal. If he has any inkling you're coming, it will mean certain death for Amy and her family."

"What do you suggest we do? Do a spell to make ourselves invisible? If you haven't noticed, we're not the most advanced police force." Robbie pointed to the outdated police cruisers. "And we certainly don't know how to do magic." He put his hand on his gun, as if to say, "We do real."

Robbie opened the door to the cop car and pointed for Billy to get in.

Billy slid into the passenger's seat. "We need to sneak attack Jake. My recommendation is to take the Deer Lane, the tiny back road behind their property. We'll all need to go through the woods. The paramedics can drive pretty far until they reach the shed. Matt needs help first. The ambulance can take him off to the hospital—they can use their sirens on Main. The rest of your team will follow me to the house. I know a route that's heavily wooded, even in winter. Jake will never see us coming."

"Great. Hiking wasn't on my agenda for the night."

"Neither was a hostage situation, but I guarantee that's what it's going to turn into once we get there."

Robbie shouted into his two-way radio, relaying the instructions to the rest of his entourage. One by one, each vehicle shut off their lights and backed up onto Main Street.

When Robbie's car was in front, they all followed close behind down Main until they reached Deer Lane. They almost missed the sign, which was completely snow covered, as was the narrow and rocky dirt road.

Billy had traveled down Deer Lane many times when he needed to access their property from the back. It was tough enough for a plow to get down the road in this kind of weather, let alone four cop cars and an ambulance. But at least Matt would have a chance to be saved and Jake wouldn't know what hit him.

CHAPTER SIXTEEN

WITH TWO MINUTES remaining on the timer, the doorknob turned. Jake thought it through this go around and he locked up the house.

"Jake, it's Billy. Let me in."

Jake looked through the peephole and sure enough, Billy Campbell was standing on the front porch.

"Why should I do that?"

"Because, I'm the last piece to your puzzle."

"What would possess you to come back here? What's in it for you?"

"Amy." He realized his mistake and quickly corrected himself with, "Amelia. I'm willing to sacrifice myself for her. I know that's stupid and I'm going to lose, but I have to try."

He was right. He would lose, and he was the last person who needed to be in the house that night. Locked in with Jake Grayson. He wanted all of them in his grasp. Once he had them, he would kill them one by one.

"Be careful what you wish for, Mr. Campbell."

Jake opened the door and Billy entered. Jake threw him

up against the wall, a gun in his back. "One wrong move and you're dead. Got it?"

"Got it."

Jake dragged Billy over to his backpack were he pulled out some rope and another pair of handcuffs. He held the gun to Billy's chest as he pushed him onto the floor. The cuffs were too small for Billy, so Jake tied his wrists together with rope instead. Then he ripped off Billy's vest, obviously loaded with weapon and hurled him across the floor.

Jake slipped on Billy's vest. "Thanks for the present. I wasn't expecting a Christmas gift."

The timer on Jake's watch went off. "Damn women." He yelled to the bathroom door. "Your time's up, buttercup."

There was no answer. Jake felt his palms get sweaty and for a brief second he feared he had made a huge error in judgment by letting Amelia go to the bathroom alone. But he had checked the room. There was no way she could get out. All of a sudden, his mind raced with another concern. What if something happened to her? Silly, he thought. But deep down inside he did care for the woman. If anything was going to happen to her, it would be by his hand, when he decided. He wouldn't allow it any other way.

"Amelia, come out. I gave you eight minutes." He tried to open the door, but she had locked it. "Damn it, Amelia. Open the door or I'll break it down. I know you don't like me when I'm angry, so don't anger me. Open the damn door!"

"Need some help?" Billy asked from across the room.

Jake didn't, but he figured he might as well put the buffoon to good use while he was still alive. He lifted him up off the ground. "I need you to break the door down. Amelia's in there and she's not responding." Billy would work for Amelia.

Billy looked down at his hands and feet. "A little difficult all tied up."

"Too bad. Figure it out."

"Fine, move out of the way."

Even better, Jake thought. He didn't have to exert himself or get his hands dirty. Billy would do all the work for him.

Jake stepped aside willingly. Billy took a few steps back and then ran full force into the bathroom door, attacking it like it was his mortal enemy. The doorframe cracked and the door loosened. Jake yanked hard and the door swung open wide.

Amelia was gone.

Jake stood there, astonished for a few seconds. "Where is she?" His voice rose in staccato form. "Where is Amelia? Where did she go?"

Billy stood there looking stunned. He shook his head. "I have no idea."

Jake's temper was encapsulating him again. The wrath that often made him lose control threatened to take over. He was about to take it all out on Billy when the slanted rug caught his eye. On an angle from its prior straight position, a corner of metal appeared.

Jake fell to his knees on the bathroom floor. He ripped the rug up and threw it out into the hallway.

"What is this?" Jake understood exactly what he was looking at. He couldn't believe how stupid he had been to trust Amelia. He should have checked for a trap like this before he let her in the bathroom alone. Better yet, he should have let her piss her pants.

He turned to Billy. "You're in on this, aren't you?"

Billy backed up and lifted his restrained hands. "I've never seen that door before in my life."

Jake wanted to blame the loser, but something told him Billy was being honest. Still, Jake couldn't rely on his own judgment. Clearly drinking was a bad idea on his part this evening. It had clouded his thinking. He was making mistakes.

Well, there was one mistake Amelia wouldn't be able to fix.

Jake stood up slowly. He smoothed his hair back, and then used the hand towel to wipe the sweat from his brow. Checking himself in the mirror, he was pleased.

He made his way to Billy until they were nose to nose.

"Listen to me, you worthless piece of garbage. You tell my Amelia, in whatever way you need to; she has exactly five minutes to show up on this doorstep. Or one by one, I promise to murder every person in this room, starting with her dear, old Dad. Got it?"

Billy's eyes darted to Richard, who stood alert. He shook his head, either to ask Jake not to kill him or to tell Billy not to bring his precious daughter back into this already doomed scenario.

Jake set his watch timer once again. "Five minutes."

"How am I supposed to find her?"

"That's not my problem. But if you don't, Richard dies."

Jake made his way back to the recliner, walking his easy, leisurely stroll. It felt good for him to be back in the saddle. Everyone's lives depended on Amelia. She wouldn't let them down. He was familiar enough with her to get that fact right.

Billy maneuvered his way outside. Jake wasn't concerned. Her ex-boyfriend wouldn't go far. Who cared if he did anyway? He needed Amelia. Everyone else was going to die, either before she arrived or after.

He listened as Billy wailed into the night, howling like a

wolf. "Amelia, come back. Amelia, where are you? We need you."

Jake flipped the recliner open, leaned back and took a little break. It would be mayhem from here on out and he needed to rest up.

CHAPTER SEVENTEEN

"WHAT SHOULD I do?" I was panicking. I had heard what Jake said and he wasn't bluffing. Billy's wire had worked perfectly—too perfectly.

"You're wired up and armed. Go in. We're right behind you. Don't do anything stupid. We can't protect you if you do something stupid, you understand?"

"I understand." I had every intention of doing something stupid, no matter what Robbie said. I was armed, like he said. What was the point of being armed if I couldn't protect myself?

It was as though he could read my mind. "The only reason we're letting you in there with your gun is because, quite frankly, I know you. And the last thing I want is for you to go into a situation like this unarmed. If you use it to scare him, or in self-defense—if it is, in fact, self-defense— you might have a chance to escape imprisonment. And, I have no doubt if we barrel in there, all three of your family members, in addition to Billy, will go down in a barrage of gunfire. That's not how we want this to end, you hear me?"

"I do." I didn't want it to end that way either. Baiting me

was smart on Jake's part and the police's part. Besides, he was planning to kill my father, and I wasn't going to allow it.

"But, we will...I repeat, we will shoot Jake to kill the minute we get a clean shot. Whatever you do, stay away from him."

"I will. Listen, I have to go before I run out of time."

Robbie patted me on the back. "Get on going. We'll hear you on the wire."

As I sprinted through the deep snow, using all of my energy, Billy screamed my name in the distance. My panicked heart hoped I'd get there according to Jake's clock. He wanted me more than he wanted to commit murder. Hell, maybe he wanted both, but I was definitely the one thing he wanted most. He was going to great, and illegal, lengths to prove it.

With every holler, Billy was acting a part. But underneath his choreographed request, there lived a real desperation in his voice. He must have gotten a glimpse of the madman that was Jake Grayson, even madder than the crazy man who was prepared to shoot and hang the gentle souls in my family.

Despite the terrifying prospects of what could go wrong, a part of me was mortified I would accept someone so damaged into my life. Billy knew I had made such a terrible choice for myself. I don't know why I cared what he thought. It was more likely that I didn't have the stomach to deal with why I cared at all. A part of me, a part hidden far beneath the surface, still loved my first love.

Billy waved his bound hands the best he could from the porch. "Hurry."

I did. I sprinted right past him and burst through the front door, pulling up short in front of Jake.

Jake was staring at his beeping watch. "Well, Amelia. You managed to come through, as I suspected you would."

"I'm here. What do you want?"

"You, of course." He took a few steps further. "But, unfortunately, you were too slow."

"What's that supposed to mean?" I moved closer to my father and Billy followed suit.

Jake pulled out a gun and pointed it at Billy. My father's eyes grew wide and he began to moan. Kate and my mom mirrored his panicked response.

"Don't do anything stupid, Jake. I came to you. I listened. Please, put down the gun and I'll do whatever you want me to do."

"Of course, you will. But, first I need to make good on my promise. If I don't you'll never be able to trust me. I won't be a man of my word. And, quite frankly, Amelia, you deserve that much in a man."

Jake kicked the chair out from under my father. I saw my dad's feet slip off the seat. His body tilted slightly and it looked like he was falling in slow motion. As I watched the noose tighten around his neck, it was as if I froze. All I could do was launch myself at my father in an effort to save him. But, Billy reacted first.

With bound hands, Billy caught my father in mid-air, seconds before the noose was going to break his neck.

That's when I saw Jake aim at Billy. I pulled my gun out in record time and did the same; only my gun was pointed at Jake. He saw my reaction and as he was pulling the trigger, he flinched. The bullet grazed Billy but landed in the wall behind him.

I tried to get a better shot at Jake, but missed entirely. Jake ducked off to the side and almost fell, but he regained his balance. He darted into the bathroom.

He was headed to the basement.

"Are you okay?" I asked Billy.

He nodded. "I'm fine."

"You know I'm going after him."

"No, Amy. Let the cops handle it this time. He's going to kill you."

The wild sirens outside told me the wires were still working. A group of police officers swarmed the front lawn and were headed to the house. "It's my mess to fix. Get my family out of here fast and safely."

I turned and went after Jake, slipping beneath the surface of the bathroom floor and into the basement. One of two old lovers was going to live and the other one was going to die.

CHAPTER EIGHTEEN

ONCE I WAS far enough down the ladder to clear the opening, I locked the door above my head. When my feet hit the basement floor, I heard the plethora of police stomping around above me.

It was fully dark. I couldn't see a thing. It looked exactly like it did when I escaped earlier, only this time, I had to worry about Jake attacking me. He could be anywhere.

I spun around and looked for his shadow anywhere. For all I knew, Jake had fled out the back of the house.

"Where are you?" My voice echoed in the darkness. "There are police everywhere. You're not getting out of here alive. You might as well surrender. They will shoot to kill you if you don't."

A sinister laugh came from the far left corner of the basement. "If they shoot, none of us are getting out of here alive."

"You're wrong." I followed the sound of his voice. "The police are bringing my family to safety. You can't hurt them anymore, Jake. It's just me and you now."

"You don't understand, Amelia." Jake stepped out of the darkness. "If anyone shoots—you, me, even the cops—we will all blow up like the fourth of July. Of course, I have no problem with death. I've never been afraid to die. But you, on the other hand, I believe you don't share my blasé attitude on the topic. Even if you did, you wouldn't sacrifice your loved ones for your ego."

My gun was pointed directly at his head. "You're crazy and you're not going to get the best of me this time. I'm not opposed to pulling the trigger right this minute." I didn't want to kill anyone, but I would kill him if I had to.

"You won't do it." Jake walked over to the utility area, which housed the electrical panel, hot water heater, washer and dryer. He grabbed what was left of a black hose. "You see this, here? Do you know what it is?"

I wasn't in the mood to play his games, but I wanted to hear what he had to say. "Get to the point, or you're going to die."

The bastard laughed at me. My finger was shaking on the trigger. It took everything I had inside of me not to kill him right there on the spot. Even if part of what he was saying was true, I needed to hear it all. I wasn't about to take a chance with the lives of everyone I loved merely to satisfy my urge to murder the psychopath.

"You see, Amelia. I'm smart. And more clever than you think. And there's no way in hell I'd risk losing you to another man. As the saying goes, if I can't have you, no one can...right?" Jake held the hose in his hand. "This, my love, is the gas line." He waved it in the air. "And, as you can see, I've severed it. Since we've been down here chitchatting away, the basement has been filling up with natural gas. As you know, natural gas is highly flammable. In fact, even one tiny spark of any kind will cause a massive explosion." Jake paused, examining the hose intently before letting it go. "So, unless you want to blow yourself up, along with the rest of your family, and your old lover, you'll put that bomb fuse down."

My arm was shaking uncontrollably. If he was telling the truth, and my gut told me he was, we were all utterly screwed. I carefully moved my finger away from the trigger. I didn't want to surrender, but I also didn't want to kill all of us. I prayed the police were still listening to my wire and had heard everything Jake said. Otherwise, we could all inadvertently be turned into ashes.

"Never." I had no strategy except to try to keep him at bay until the cops took action, which was only a matter of time. A gun in my hand put me in control, even if I had no intention of using it.

"Fine. We'll do this your way." He pulled his gun out and pointed it into the air. "Shooting you, shooting the ceiling...no matter. We die either way." He took a few steps closer to me. "I know you, Amelia. You may be willing to kill me, but you have absolutely no intention of committing mass murder." He put the butt of the gun to his temple. "Even if I kill myself, you and your family will die. No matter what happens, we all die. Not only one of us...all of us." He dropped the gun to his side. "That's precisely why I'm not afraid of you and your useless gun. You'll never shoot it."

He came even closer until he stood within inches of my gun. "Give it to me, Amelia. We can do this nicely, or you can get hurt in the process. Either way, I'm leaving with you as my hostage, or neither of us are leaving here alive. Your choice."

There was no choice to be made. Jake was right. I would never fire the gun. But, he would. He planned to kill anyone in the vicinity of my childhood home.

The amplified sound of the police boomed through the house. "Jake Grayson, we have the premises surrounded. Come out with your hands up, or we'll come in after you. We're giving you to the count of ten. One..."

I couldn't chance an altercation. If the police infiltrated our house, Jake would blow us all up.

"Three..."

It was time I gave up.

"Five..."

Jake grabbed the barrel of my gun and I released my grip. I said nothing.

"Seven..."

"That's my girl." He wrapped his arm around my neck and shoved his gun against my head. "Don't do anything stupid." Then Jake dragged me across the basement.

"Nine..."

On the count of ten we were above ground, surrounded by tens of cops with guns pointed at us. They wouldn't take a shot at him unless it was a clear shot, and it wasn't even close. Jake had positioned me directly in front of him, with his gun right up against my head.

It was my chance to speak up and try to save us. "Don't shoot. He gassed our house. It'll explode on impact. Please."

I saw Robbie in front and he nodded. I didn't know what their plan was, and something told me they didn't have a plan. They were small town police officers. Nothing like this had ever happened before. Training or not, being in a hostage situation like this was the most unexpected crime to ever hit Shady Knolls. They were most certainly playing the situation minute to minute. It was crystal clear to me that I was the only one who was going to get us out of this situation alive.

"You heard the woman," Jake said calmly. "Drop your weapons and let us go."

Another officer, likely Robbie's superior stepped forward. "Listen to me, Jake. At this point, you haven't killed anyone. Matt is doing fine. The rest of the Montgomery family, along with Billy Campbell, are safe and unharmed. We realize you're under a tremendous amount of pressure. You're someone who needs professional help. But, you're not a criminal. If you let Amelia go, we can work this all out. I promise to convince the Montgomery family not to press charges, as long as you seek treatment. Honestly, it's a win-win for everybody." He paused for the proposal to sink in.

Jake's grip on me lightened and for a moment it seemed as though he might be considering the opportunity.

The officer went on. "However, if you choose to ignore my proposition and continue holding Amelia hostage, I'll have no choice but to take action."

Jake squeezed me tighter. He didn't like to be threatened by anyone, let alone an officer of the law. In Jake's eyes, he was above the law.

Jake sniggered. "You bottom-feeding parasites. Do you think a man of my stature is ignorant enough to listen to your uneducated offerings? I'm not playing a game here. This is my life. And here, is the love of my life. And whether or not you agree with our decision to be together, I will have my Amelia one way or another. So, act if you must. Do your worst, because if you kill me, you're killing her as well. Take your chances...but I don't think you have the guts to do a damn thing."

My legs slid in the snow as he dragged me backwards to the front of the house. "Please, let me go. They're going to kill you, Jake."

"Shut up. This isn't about you. You're as stupid as they are." He chuckled. "I don't know why I'm surprised. Shady Knolls isn't exactly where smart people are bred."

My blood was boiling over. This bastard wasn't going to get away with what he did and kidnap me in the process. There was no way I could let his plan come to fruition.

The cops followed after us, guns on Jake and me. "You won't get far, Jake. We'll give you another minute to decide. You let her go, and we'll let you live. We'll work out a deal. But if you try to take her, you'll die."

I fully accepted what I had to do. I would be risking my life to do it, but what choice did I have?

I relaxed my body. Jake kept the gun pressed to my temple and his arm around my neck. I could tell he wasn't trying to hurt me, oddly enough. His goal was to get me to the car where he could take me. I would never be free again.

There was no way the cops were going to shoot him, no matter what they said. Jake had assumed as much early on, and it's precisely the reason he had no fear.

When we reached Jake's car, the cops were still following us closely, all the while pleading with Jake to let me go. By that time, he had figured them out and he was more confident than ever.

Focused on getting me in the car, he maneuvered the driver's door open and shoved me into the other side. All the while, he had the gun pointed at my head.

However, he was confident to a fault. And for a brief second, his head turned to pull the door closed.

That's when I saw my chance. I was prepared to fight to the death, and death was what it had come to.

I shoved my right hand down my blouse, and ripped out my last resort. I knocked Jake's hand out of the way and shoved the butt of my thirty-eight special into the back of his head.

I whispered, "God forgive me." And I pulled the trigger.

CHAPTER NINETEEN

THE BREEZE BLEW Amy's hair away from her face, and Billy caught a sparkle in her eye.

"Look! Isn't it gorgeous?"

Billy hugged her a little tighter than normal and kissed her on the cheek. "Blue's my new favorite color."

The fireworks display lit up the sky over the Jersey Shore as the Montgomery family huddled in awe.

Over six months passed since Amelia had killed Jake, and Billy had been by her side the whole time. She was still in therapy, but doing great. Even better than she was while dating Jake, according to her family's notice. She was damaged, but happy. And, most importantly, she was free.

Every member of the Montgomery family had survived. They were a little damaged but much stronger. Matt got to the hospital on Christmas Eve by the narrowest of margins. He had lost a lot of blood, but thankfully his blood type was a common one and after several transfusions, he recovered as if unharmed. The bullet was removed and he proudly wore his scar, as only Matty would.

Richard had suffered a mild heart attack that same

fateful night. Test results after he was rescued showed the damage, but he too, had recovered quite nicely.

Caroline had made it through the debacle with no issues at all. However, through follow up testing, doctors discovered she had early stage thyroid cancer, which had explained her previous weight loss and fatigue. After her surgery to remove the tumor, and a few treatments she was doing very well and her prognosis was good.

Kate, on the other hand, had suffered the deepest emotional wounds out of all of them. After all she had been through with the miscarriages, the night Jake Grayson terrorized their family had almost sent her over the edge. After giving birth, albeit early, to their daughter, Melanie, her name a spin on Amelia's nickname Mel, the one who had saved them all, Kate was progressing wonderfully.

Billy felt he gained the most from the tragedy of the prior year's Christmas Eve. He had been unexpectedly reunited with the love of his life and his world had become complete. No matter what he and Amy had to go through to get to that point, Billy was truly grateful.

In many ways, both Billy and Amy were grateful to Jake for their happiness, as crazy as it seemed to them.

As it turned out, Billy and Amy were engaged with a baby on the way. Their son was due on Christmas Eve. They decided to name him Kristian, a name that reminded them of Christmas. It was exactly what everyone needed to ensure the holidays were synonymous with love and not with pain. New memories were going to be made, ones full of family and focused on living in peace.

"I'm thrilled we bought this place," Amy said. "I've always wanted to live at the beach."

"Me too," Billy said.

After Amy decided to change careers and move back to

New Jersey to become a residential real estate agent, she had been incredibly successful. They were able to keep Billy's house in Shady Knolls, and purchase a beautiful house on the beach. They had the best of both worlds.

As the Montgomery family, and soon-to-be Campbell family, gathered close for the fourth of July fireworks finale, they all linked arms and pulled each other close.

It was the beginning of a beautiful life for all of them.

THE END

Get a taste of another story by Kristina Rienzi, *Again*. The first chapter follows.

Chapter One

LUCY PRACTICED HER venomous script, role-playing with the vacant chair opposite her. "Today...is your last day. Today is your last...day. Today is...your last day."

As the human resources director, Lucy Matheson wore a plethora of hats at work, many of which she would have preferred to toss. Especially the dark one, the hat that required she fire people with professionalism and grace. She rolled her eyes at the thought. There was no such thing as gracefully firing someone. No matter how one lost their job, it was never pretty.

Lucy straightened, cleared her throat, and then suited her energy up for the person without emotions. She sharpened her tone and demeanor until the message sounded clear, concise, and indisputably final. "Today is your last day." She smiled to herself, pleased with her ability to pull it off.

Tightening the silk scarf around her neck, Lucy recalled the recent meeting with her boss, who also happened to be the CEO and namesake of the firm.

"As you know, once Edmon Enterprises acquired this company, our first order of business was to clean house." Mr. Edmon adjusted his tie as he spoke. "The first week we took over, we promptly walked most of the employees, one by one, straight out the front door. That day wasn't one of my proudest moments, but it was essential to the future of our business. It wasn't personal. It's still hard to believe our mass layoff was six months ago already. Many times it feels like yesterday." He closed his eyes and shook his head at the memory.

Lucy remained silent. There was no easy way to agree or disagree with him. She had heard all about the terrible day in the company's history and was very grateful she had not been around at that point.

"As I'm certain you've heard, management wasn't prepared to handle the mayhem that ensued from the remaining staff after that massacre. No one was productive for weeks. They spent their days crying, or gossiping, or calling out sick in protest. Rumors started spreading like wildfire around here. The employees left behind were in an uproar. And I suppose I can't blame them one bit."

Lucy offered her support. "You did the right thing. I know that's not always popular with everyone, but it is business, not personal, like you said."

He pursed his lips. "Well, that may be true, but look at it from their point of view. Hard-working folks were forced to sit back and watch helplessly as their coworkers, their friends, carried cardboard boxes filled with years' worth of belongings out to their cars."

"It must have been a difficult time." Lucy gave him her best sympathetic look. She had been hired shortly after that incident, essentially walking into the aftermath of a war zone. It hadn't been an easy transition for anyone to have a new hire show up amongst a sea of terminations.

Mr. Edmon continued. "Your accomplishments in the Human Resources industry are very impressive. Did you know your nickname behind closed doors is *The Terminator?*"

Lucy nodded. Her face warmed. She was compelled to explain her often-misguided nickname. "It's not something I brag about, but yes, it's a part of my job that I take quite seriously." An apologetic half-smile was all she could muster.

"And you're damned good at it, Ms. Matheson." Mr. Edmon's expression lit up, as though he were proud of her. Then it quickly turned serious. "That's why you're the one who's going to handle Edmon Enterprise's final termination."

Lucy scrunched her face in confusion. "I'm sorry if I misunderstood, but I thought we eliminated all of the positions from Volger Industries already?"

"That's mostly true." Mr. Edmon shrugged. "However, given the sensitive circumstances when a corporate firm acquires a family business, we made an exception for one employee."

Tatiana. The name came to Lucy like a tsunami. How had she forgotten? A sharp pain electrified her chest. Her hand flew to her heart. The twinge of an impending panic attack always rocked her world, even more so after her parents' unexpected death one year ago. She took a deep breath in recovery and tried to clear her mind, but the reality of her assignment didn't sit well with her.

Tatiana Volger, the daughter of the firm's founder and lone survivor of Volger Industries, was still employed. And she was untouchable.

Despite the distaste of the undertaking, Mr. Edmon was giving Lucy an opportunity to prove herself. Decidedly, she was ready to step up to the plate and swing.

To continue reading, pick up *Again* at your favorite retailer.

ALSO BY KRISTINA RIENZI

Ensouled Series

Choosing Evil

Breaking Evil

Other Stories

Among Us

Winter Road

Luring Shadows

Again

Train Girl

To Preserve, Protect and Defend

Twisted

30 Shades of Dead

Audiobooks

Among Us

Winter Road

ABOUT THE AUTHOR

Kristina Rienzi is a Jersey Shore-based new adult thriller author, certified professional coach, and the former president of Sisters in Crime-Central Jersey. An INFJ who dreams beyond big, Kristina encourages others (and herself) to embrace the unknown through her stories. When she's not writing or drinking wine, Kristina is spoiling her baby girl (and two fur-babies), dissecting true crime stories, singing (and dancing) to Yacht Rock Radio, or rooting for the WVU Mountaineers. She believes in all things paranormal, a closet full of designer bags, weekly manicures, the Law of Attraction, aliens, angels, and the value of a graduate degree in psychology. Her debut audiobook, *Among Us* was featured on Audible's ACX University and is an Audible Editors Select pick.

Visit her online at
KristinaRienzi.com

 facebook.com/KristinaRienzi

twitter.com/kristinarienzi

instagram.com/kristinarienzi

amazon.com/author/kristinarienzi

9 780996 972123